Whispering Bricks

Stories of Love, Loss, and Friendship from IIMA

SIDDHARTHA BHASKER

FiNGERPRINT!

Published by
FiNGERPRINT!
An imprint of Prakash Books India Pvt. Ltd.

113/A, Darya Ganj, New Delhi-110 002,
Tel: (011) 2324 7062 – 65, Fax: (011) 2324 6975
Email: info@prakashbooks.com/sales@prakashbooks.com

www.facebook.com/fingerprintpublishing
www.twitter.com/FingerprintP
www.fingerprintpublishing.com

Copyright © 2021 Prakash Books India Pvt. Ltd.
Copyright Text © Siddhartha Bhasker

All rights reserved. No part of this publication may be reproduced, stored in a retrieval system or transmitted in any form or by any means, electronic, mechanical, photocopying, recording or otherwise (except for mentions in reviews or edited excerpts in the media) without the written permission of the publisher.

ISBN: 978 93 5440 290 6

Processed & printed in India

Dedicated

to

WIMWIans…

∽∾

CONTENTS

Introduction	7
Placements and Society	9
The Last Flight to Chennai	17
Mr Peace in PGP2	39
Four Walls Don't Make a Classroom	47
Reunion	55
Angel of Love	63
The Deadly Time of 1:45 pm	71
Ixx Globe	79
Presenting Ravana	85
Abhi and Rhea	93
Serendipity	99
Bite Me	113
Chakru Clears His Debts	125
DiscF	135
The Taxi Driver	147
Acknowledgement	*157*
About the Author	*159*

Introduction

IIM Ahmedabad is known for its success stories. If you browse through Google news, you will inevitably find that somebody or the other from this institute is always present in the newsfeed. But what goes on within those red brick walls of IIMA? This collection of short stories will answer just that question.

The title of this book comes from an article I read about Louis Kahn, the famous architect who designed the campus. He was called 'The Brick Whisperer'. And the walls that he created have been witness to countless stories and innumerable whispers. Think of a person leaning against one of these walls and listening to the stories they have to tell ... well, this book is the voice of that person, bringing those stories across to you in the hope that they don't die ...

These stories were collected from the entering batch of 2012-15 at IIMA. Asking MBA grad students to write stories is like pitching your ideas to a VC for funds. In other words, they, the students, are busy, opinionated, and are always looking for a value for their resources. Writing a story does not really fit into their scheme of things. And so it was that things lingered and floundered. A lot of promises went unfulfilled. And it took three years to put together the stories in this collection. Publishing this book took a few more years due to unforeseen circumstances, including my struggles with schizophrenia and the COVID-19 pandemic. But now that I see it in its final form, it gives me a sense of fulfilment. Was all this effort and wait worth it? I can't answer that question. Not just yet. For it is up to you, the readers, to decide that.

Siddhartha Bhasker
Sonipat, April 2021

Placements and Society

ASHISH RANJAN

"It was a brilliant lecture, man. I mean I never thought this topic would have so many dimensions," Archana said as they came out of the social entrepreneurship class.

"Well, it's just a lecture. Let's not make too much of it," the ever pessimistic Rajesh shot back.

"Do you guys want to go out for tea and snacks?" Harpreet asked, keeping one hand on his tummy.

"Yes, that's a good idea. In any case, we have a break till the 11:55 am class," said Tapas.

They walked towards the main gate. Archana, a short and petite woman who always looked at the brighter side of things, was a little ahead of the rest. Rajesh, the perfect antidote to her, was tall and slim and had big brown eyes that looked deceptively dopey. Tapas was quiet and shy, and mostly walked with his head pointed downwards. Harpreet was big and heavy and was, almost always, hungry. They had all belonged to the same section in their first year and had become good friends over classes, assignments, and internships. Now that they were about to pass out, the bonds of friendship had only strengthened.

"Yesterday, one of these stupid birds made me a target." Rajesh looked up in vengeance at the trees near the Harvard Steps. Archana giggled.

"You must have committed some sin against them. Poor birds," Archana said as Rajesh scoffed at her. "I always put a bowl of water in my balcony for these poor creatures. That is why they have probably spared me till now," she added.

"The social service lady!" Rajesh mocked. "The future Mother Teresa!"

"*Rehne do*. Let it be. I do not want to become any Mother Teresa-Weresa. Just making a small contribution to society would be enough for me."

"Are you actually serious about your plan?" Harpreet asked.

"Yes, I am," Archana said.

The plan that Harpreet was referring to was

Archana's desire to start a unique educational venture for children from poor families. Her mother was a noted social service worker who ran a chain of schools for kids from the slums of Navi Mumbai. Archana planned to overhaul the teaching methods used in these schools through the use of new technologies in education. The only thorn, and a big one at that, in her decision-making, was the attractive Pre-Placement Offer (PPO) she had already bagged from a big consulting firm. It would be a rather bold decision to choose one over the other.

"She is ultimately going to join the consulting firm, I am telling you. All this social service idea is a temporary fad." Rajesh had a devilish smile on his face.

"And what makes you think so?" Archana stopped and stood with her hands on her hips, staring at him.

"Come on! Are you telling me that you would leave a 25-lakh package just to work for these poor kids? I mean it's not impossible, but it's not as easy as you think it is either. Your decision looks too simplistic, too idealistic to me."

"Rajesh, why do you even take these social entrepreneurship courses if these ideas look too simplistic, too idealistic to you?" Archana demanded and started walking away from him.

"Guys, let's think practically," Tapas interjected. "I think Rajesh is right when he says that Archana's decision looks too simple. I mean look at your opportunity cost, Archana!"

"If everyone thinks this way, then nobody is ever going to do anything about the poor simply because the people who are in a position to help will always have a higher opportunity cost!"

They had crossed the main gate and were across the road from the tea stall around which a small crowd had assembled. College-going students sipping tea and talking, idle men staring vacantly at the road in front of them, two cows munching on the grass, a few dogs lolling around, and some small half-naked children going through the waste bin next to the tea stall in search for anything that could be salvaged and eaten, occupied the footpath in spite of the glaring sun.

Rajesh pointed at the half-naked children and said, "They are the kind of people you want to help, is it?"

"Yes. Can we talk of something else now?" Archana replied as they began to carefully cross the road. At that time of the day, the traffic on the road was quite heavy.

"Yes, I think you guys should stop harassing her," Harpreet said.

"We are not harassing anybody, just discussing things," Rajesh retorted.

"Why don't we talk about Tapas then? He won the first prize in a competition today. A lakh rupees!"

"What? Wow!" Archana exclaimed, turning to Tapas. "What was the competition about?"

"It was the development of a business idea for the agro-business project," Tapas answered.

"*Sahi*. Nice! So, is there a party?"

"Yes. Yes. Whenever you guys say."

They had reached the tea stall. The owner smiled at them as he put some sugar into the boiling tea on the stove. Harpreet walked up to the street vendor right next to the tea stall and pointing at the pouches of packaged water the man was selling, he asked, "Are these water pouches all right?" He picked up a pouch and looked at it dubiously. "I am feeling thirsty in this heat." When the others assured him that the pouches were indeed all right, Harpreet bought a couple of them from the street vendor. The ice-cold pouches were a relief to hold in the heat. He drank two of them and offered the rest to the others who refused. He thought of returning the remaining pouches to the street vendor and asking for his money back. But then he remembered the one black and one red eye of the vendor and thought it better not to turn back again.

"What do I do with these pouches?"

"Do some social service. Give them to those street kids," Rajesh suggested.

"Haha!" Harpreet laughed and then suddenly stopped. "Oh! Not a bad idea actually."

The street kids were already approaching him, and in a smooth transaction, Harpreet handed the remaining pouches over to them without a single word being spoken between the two parties.

"They could have said thank you or at least taken the pouches with a smile," Rajesh cribbed as the children ran back.

"They don't have water to drink! How can you expect manners?" Archana asked, exasperated.

"Manners are inbuilt," Rajesh answered, shrugging his shoulders. "Anyway, are we having something to eat?"

"Yes, this guy makes tasty bread pakoras. Let's have some."

While waiting for the bread pakoras, Tapas called their attention to a peculiar incident that was taking place just a couple of feet away from them. The kids who had taken the pouches of water from Harpreet were busy draining the water into a small hole in the road. They kept at it meticulously until every last drop of water from the pouches had been extracted. Once done, all of them ran away from the spot, throwing satisfied looks at each other.

"Leakage, my friends, is the villain of our public distribution system," Tapas said.

The bread pakoras arrived just then, and they all turned away from the pool of water and focussed on the food in front of them.

"Delicious!" Harpreet gave his judgement in a split second.

"But now I am feeling thirsty. Need to buy some water," Tapas said.

"The water Harpreet donated had a higher opportunity cost, I would say," Rajesh said, turning back towards the vendor to buy four pouches of water.

No one responded to Rajesh's comment, and the four friends made their way through the bread pakoras and the tea in silence. As they paid the bill a little while later and turned to go back for their 11.55 am class, Tapas asked lazily, "What do you guys think will be the highest package our batch bags?"

Archana, who had been quiet for some time now, said, "I think around—" She broke off mid-sentence and stopped short. "Hey! Look!" she shouted as the rest of them turned back to look at her questioningly.

The kids were coming back towards the pool of water. Leading the pack were a little boy and a girl, and following them in line were five street dogs. The whole group stopped near the pool and the kids immediately set about clearing the space for the dogs. The little girl then signalled to the dogs to come forward and drink the water. And the dogs did so, with palpable satisfaction, the children laughing and encouraging them as they lapped up the water. As the last of the dogs quenched its thirst and walked away, the little girl looked up at the four friends with a shy smile on her face, as if saying thank you.

"Now let's talk about a higher opportunity cost!" Archana chuckled as she waited for a speeding car to pass before crossing the road.

The Last Flight to Chennai

ASHWIN RAVICHANDRAN

~~~

It was the phone call that changed an evening filled with the prospect of completing the presentation for his Marketing-I class and reading three twenty-something pages of cases, into a night of utter despair and helplessness. When the deafening sound of the popular AR Rahman song which was his ringtone, shook him from his listlessness, he picked up the phone and looked at the name of the caller; it was his father. While it wasn't unusual for his parents to call him once a day, they usually called him later in the night, when they knew he would be done with his classes for the day. A part of his brain noted that it was a rather unlikely time for his parents to have called him. But as is the case with all passing thoughts, he dismissed it and picking up the call, said "Hello!" with a grin on his face. All it took was nine full seconds for his lips to let go of that enthusiastic grin and for his face to lose all colour.

When he put the phone down, his hands involuntarily closed the case material (casemat) open on the study table in front of him, while his legs searched for his slippers under the table. He got up without meaning to do so. To remain sitting seemed unbearable. Like a blind man, he followed his mind and heart, both of which were some 2,000 kms away in Chennai. His head was filled with the sound of that familiar, booming laughter that had marked his childhood, and his heart, his heart was remembering the gentle love and the big kiss that had enveloped him every time he had gone back home. He knew that he had to go home. That he had to fix things at once. Say goodbye. But his legs were like glue, incapable of obeying his commands. So he stood there in the middle of his hostel room, a boy who didn't quite know where he was or what he should do next, until managing to finally pull his senses together, he realised he needed to book a flight ticket.

The laptop was powered on in a flash. The Chrome browser, though, was not quite as fast. When the web page finally opened, he searched hurriedly for the next flight to Chennai. There was one that left at 10:15 pm. The time at the bottom of the laptop screen read 5:33 pm. A good three hours to reach the airport that was more than 10 kms from the campus. If he factored in the time it would take for him to pack, inform the necessary people about his urgent need to go home, and also deal with the traffic that he was bound to face at that time of the day, he could just about make it to the airport with the slimmest of buffers. Just as he was about to select the flight and book the ticket, a tiny notification popped up on the screen. It was a mail from the Post Graduate Program (PGP) office, which looked after the academic affairs of the MBA students. His mouse clicked on the notification of its own accord, as though an invisible hand had made it do that. The mail contained the seating arrangements for the Slot 2 exams of the first-year students that were to begin on Thursday. And that was when he suddenly realised that it was a Monday. The exams were to start in a little more than sixty hours. It was at that moment that the naked truth hit him with full force and the first tear rolled down his cheek. His guide, his confidant, his rock, his grandfather had passed away. It was as if everyone in the world had died and he was left all alone.

***

It was on 16 June 2013 that he had stood proudly on the famous Harvard Steps for the first time. His dad had not wasted a moment to click a picture of his son there even as his mother, standing at the foot of the steps, had urged them to hurry. "Let's go check out your room, Gautham," she had called out.

Slowly, they had walked towards Dorm 24, situated in the New Campus. It had only been the three of them that day as his grandfather had pulled out of the trip at the last minute. A long-standing issue with his grandmother's right kneecap had ensured that she would spend the weekend at home, nursing the knee with a hot-water bottle over it, and his grandfather would never even dream of leaving his wife alone in that state. Gautham had been extremely disappointed. The one person he had really wanted to show his new campus to was the 84-year-old man who had raised him and given him the knowledge that no MBA degree could ever impart.

Three weeks into the course and he had realised why the institute was considered the best in the country. Innumerable cases, assignments, quizzes, and club meetings later, he knew he was no longer in control of his life. He knew that he had 24 hours in a day. But what he did not know was how these 24 hours were being spent. The hours just seemed to all whizz right by him. In the last ten days, he had not even had a chance to talk to Lavanya, the girl he intended to marry. About thirteen months ago, both Lavanya and he had realised that they were no longer just the usual childhood friends who see each other grow and move off and away. They wanted more. And they wanted it together. He had taken the bold step of verbalising that realisation, to which she had responded instantly, and that too, positively. The past year had, in short, been one of the best years of his life. But what he needed now was a lever that he could hold onto, a lever that could literally help him catch his breath. He had always believed that peer pressure was a myth. And the institute had oh-so sweetly crushed that belief in a mere second. As the thought of the next deadline loomed before his sleep-deprived eyes, he felt a sudden urge to talk to Lavanya. It was just ten minutes past six in the evening, which meant that Lavanya would be at work, coding lines of Python scripts. Calling her at this hour would elicit no response, especially when she was already mad at him for having missed their usual Saturday night call. Moreover, it was not Lavanya's gentle love that he was looking for at the moment. He thought of his undergrad college gang. Would Vikranth, Abhinav or Satvik talk to him now and provide what he was looking for? But then again, to be honest, he himself did not know what he was looking for. He could call his mother of course. She would be busy cooking dinner, but that wouldn't keep her from talking to him. He dialled her number. But before the first ring, he cut the call. He did not want to worry his mother with his troubles. She would get bogged down by his state of mind and would then worry and fuss endlessly. No. He definitely did not want that.

Gautham looked around his room, at the shadows cast by the lamp on his table. He felt alone. He was alone. His dorm mates were all busy battling headaches of their own. And his study group was caught up in deciphering the probability problem that was due on the morrow.

As he stared at the mobile in his hand, it hit him—he knew just the person who would take his call and hear him out, who would not hesitate to scold him for his mistakes or gently guide him out of troubled waters . . . the man who could simply alleviate all his worries with a simple anecdote. Gautham dialled his grandfather's landline number.

"Hello!"

"Hello, Gautham!"

He had always admired his grandfather's ability to identify his voice. Once again, all it took was a simple, customary hello.

"How are you, *Taatha*[1]?"

---

1 Tamil word for grandfather

"I am fine here. So is your grandmother. Her knee still hurts, but I think I will resume my morning walks with her next week."

"That's great to hear."

"So, tell me Gautham . . . what is bothering you?"

"How did you know that . . ."

"I have lived through your age! And even though that was some sixty years ago, nobody really forgets those days, do they? You wouldn't have called if it hadn't been something important. Is everything okay between Lavanya and you?"

His grandfather was the only one in his family who knew about Lavanya. He was the only one with whom Gautham could talk about his relationship, his friendships, and just about everything else without a trace of embarrassment or awkwardness.

"Yes, yes, everything is all right between us. It's nothing of that sort, Taatha."

"Then what is it?"

"Well . . ."

That conversation, which lasted all of ten minutes and thirty-six seconds, brought an absolute change in his mood. Perhaps it was the deep, sonorous voice of his grandfather or maybe it was the simple anecdote from his childhood days in their ancestral village that his grandfather had narrated, whatever it was, Gautham knew as he kept the phone that he no longer had that big burden on his shoulders to weigh him down. What surprised him the most was that even though he had been unable to articulate his state of mind and the causes behind it, his grandfather had managed to relieve him of it all. Maybe he should talk to him at least once a week. Yes. That would be the best way to survive the rollercoaster of a life at IIMA.

***

Gautham sat staring at the phone in his hands, his father's words ringing in his ears, "Gautham, Taatha had a massive heart attack last night . . ." He had not really paid attention to the words that had followed: 'doctor', 'last rites', 'funeral', 'leave'. They had all whizzed past him. He could hear his mother sobbing in the background; her heartbreak was palpable even over the phone. After all, it was her father she had lost.

To him though, the man had been something very different. His grandfather had always maintained that the greatest human relationship was the one that existed between a grandparent and a child, simply because there was neither any expectation nor any commitment in that. Both parties maintained the relationship only because they liked it the most. And it had been a beautiful one indeed, the relationship between him and his Taatha. He had been more than a friend and a philosopher. He had been someone who had always waited for Gautham to open up so that eighty years of wisdom and experience could be transferred unflinchingly into his young mind.

But all that remained of his grandfather now were some memories that were both distant and indelible. A bearded face, a wrinkled hand, and the keen scrutiny of his magnificent eyes . . . little details flashed before him. Little details and the promises that he had made but never kept, like the promise to call Taatha every week. He yearned to see his grandfather one last time.

Once again, Gautham looked at the time. It was 5:48 pm. He needed to get on that flight. Home was where his heart and mind were. Just as he was about to confirm the payment on MakeMyTrip.com, a small voice reminded him about the email from the PGP office. He could leave that night and get back the very next evening, well in time for the exams on Thursday. But he had other stuff going on as well. Wednesday was the group presentation in the Marketing-I class, plus there was an assignment to be submitted for Probability and Statistics-II. Also, there was a possibility of a Financial Markets quiz happening, which he could not afford to miss. In short, he had to be here in Ahmedabad, attending all his classes and lectures and study group meetings the next day.

"Damn! Damn! Damn! Why the fuck am I stuck here in this hellhole? What's the point of pursuing a career that's supposed to take me places if it means that I can't even see Taatha one last time?!"

But even as Gautham cursed his situation, he knew what he needed to do. With a heavy heart, he called his dad again.

"Dad, I don't think I will be able to come."

"It's okay, Gautham."

"But I want to come, Dad."

"I understand."

"I want to see Taatha one last time."

"I know, *makan*[2]. But Taatha will always be with us. He would not have wanted you to miss out on your studies for anything."

"But . . ."

"It is all right, Gautham. We will give him a fitting send-off. You take care and focus on your studies. I'll call you later."

The phone call, needless to say, only made him feel worse. He wanted to go home even though he knew that that was not what his grandfather would have wanted him to do. But irrespective of whatever his father had said, he wanted to be there, lifting one

---

2   Tamil word for son

corner of the immortal coffin that was blessed to bear the weight of his grandfather. He wanted to be the one holding the torch showing the wise old man the way to the heavens above. He wanted to be the one listening to the Brahmins reciting the Vedic chants while serving those who had come to pay their final respects to his grandfather. But the harsh reality was that he could do none of those things.

He walked out of his room. He needed to talk to someone, someone who could somehow provide a solution to his quandary and could, perhaps, also magically transport him to Chennai, even if it was only for a few minutes. His dorm mates were, as was their wont, nowhere to be seen. The alarm on his mobile phone rang shrilly just then. It was time for an IIMACTS meeting. IIMACTS, which was the dramatics society of IIMA, had found a role for him in a play that was to be performed the next Friday. Which meant that he would not be able to attend the tenth day rituals of his grandfather's funeral either. Not that it mattered. It wasn't the rituals that he wanted to attend. He wanted to see his grandfather's face again.

He slowly walked towards the basement of Dorm 8, where the practice was to happen. As he crossed Cafe Tanstaafl (CT), he saw many happy faces going about their own lives, all of them comfortably oblivious to his state of mind. He tried to remember his character in the play. But even as he took the first few steps down to the basement, he wondered why he was there in the first place. This was his moment of grief and pain, a moment where he needed the companionship of solitude. Was it because acting and performing before an audience gave him a respite from the whirlwind life he led otherwise by taking him to another world altogether?

"Who knows?" he muttered to himself as his fingers grasped the doorknob of the door to the basement. He hesitated. Did he really want to escape into a theatrical world right then? No. Not when someone so important to him had left this real world. He turned back. The walk through the red-bricked arches of the old campus buildings seemed extremely long. But strangely, the bricks and the walls, they seemed to understand his loneliness. They had been there for more than forty years after all, watching many a wavering minds stumble and straighten and survive. He walked towards the Louis Kahn Plaza (LKP), now a beautiful lush green after the rains. His study group would be there. The one thing they all had in common was their love of sitting on the grass at the LKP. When he reached the LKP, he took off his sandals and felt the soft, moist grass below his feet.

Memories of walking with his grandfather in the small forest behind their ancestral house came rushing to his mind. The coconut trees, the big mango tree that rarely bore a yellow fruit, the hibiscus plant, and the banyan trees were all living embodiments of his grandfather's hobby. Gautham had learnt what it took to plant a sapling, water it devotedly, watch it grow patiently, and then pluck its first fruit and taste it, all with his grandfather right beside him. As he remembered those days, he wiped his eyes again. He had to get a grip over himself. He was going to meet his group and he didn't want to break down in front of them.

"You are early! Didn't you have your dram-soc practice?" boomed a rather accusatory voice.

It was Abhishek, his closest friend.

"Ready to do some PS?" Neeta, another study group member, asked.

Gautham looked at them in surprise. He had not realised that he had put his sandals back on and walked across the entire length of the lawns so quickly. Pulling himself together, he looked at his study group mates. Four of them were there—Abhishek, Neeta, Indra, and Manthesh. Manthesh was missing as usual.

Gautham took a deep breath. It was time to keep his sorrow to himself and get on with the work. After all, his group would be graded on the basis of their presentation. He could not afford to let them down with his bursts of grief, which would only serve as unwanted distractions. Unwillingly, he opened his PS casemat and got down to do the math.

It was almost an hour before another memory of his grandfather came into sudden focus in his mind. He remembered learning mathematics from him as a child. His grandfather was the only one who understood that getting a centum was not always the most important thing. The man had loved geometry, while Gautham had always struggled with it. He had never really been able to grasp the techniques that were meant to help him work out the areas and lengths of various polygons. And he almost always ended up failing to calculate the right area of the trapezium throughout the seventh grade. It was his grandfather who taught him geometry. Where his math teacher and his mother had failed, his grandfather succeeded. While the rest of the family had bemoaned his missing out on the divine score of a perfect hundred, his grandfather had taken him aside and chided him for worrying over a few marks. No one was more proud than his grandfather had been when he had scored that elusive centum in his final exam. At the same time, no one was as indifferent towards the number as his grandfather had been. He had said he still believed that a hundred was only a mark greater than ninety-nine and it was not worth celebrating. It was at that age, after that moment, that Gautham learned from his grandfather the need for a mental equipoise, irrespective of the outcome and the situation.

Now, as he brooded over the eighth problem of

the PS assignment, he wished his grandfather was there to help him out again. He also remembered that his grandfather hated statistics. He used to call it "the hurdle to creativity." Gautham tried to smile at the thought, but before he could stop himself, tears started streaming down his face.

"What happened, Gauti?" Abhishek asked, rather shocked at the sight.

All his study group members turned towards him now.

"Are you crying, Gauti?" Neeta asked, looking completely confused.

"He is! What's the matter?"

"All okay?"

"Of course not. Why else would he cry?"

Slowly, after taking a couple of long deep breaths, Gautham shared the news of his grandfather's demise with them even though he had promised himself that he wouldn't. But he wasn't that great at keeping promises. His revelation was met with immediate sympathy from his friends.

"Dude, you should take the flight to Chennai. We will take care of the assignments here, ya."

"Yeah, Gauti. Just go!"

"I'll come with you to the airport."

"But what if there is a CF quiz?"

"It's just a quiz, ya."

"Really? Just a quiz? He could miss out on at least three sub-grades if he misses a CF quiz!"

"Come on, man!"

"And what about the PlaceComm[3] deadline tomorrow, huh? The application needs to be handed over."

"We could submit his application. No big deal."

"No, I think Indra is right. Gauti can't afford to miss an entire day."

"Yeah. It would be way too costly."

Gautham only half heard what his friends were saying. He wiped his cheeks dry and began wondering, all over again, whether he should take the flight or not. It was 7:57 pm already. He knew he had to decide fast.

"Guys, please tell me what to do. I so want to see his face one last time. But . . ."

"Gauti, you leave right now. We will take care of the rest," Abhishek said.

"Let's go to his dorm and help him get set for the flight," Neeta suggested.

"Yeah."

"Yes."

Along with the four of them, Gautham walked back towards his dorm. As they passed Tapri, the

---

[3] Placement Committee of IIMA which manages the campus placement process.

campus tea stall, he recalled his grandfather's addiction to cardamom tea. "Tea and cardamom, two things that can instantly cleanse one's mind and soul," his grandfather would say. Suddenly, Gautham yearned for a cup of that tea.

"Wait. Guys. Let me get some tea."

His friends stopped and turned around to look at him with surprise. But he didn't wait to explain anything. They would just not understand. He walked over to the tea stall, paid for a cup of cardamom tea, and stood there, sipping it. It tasted sweet and heavy with all the milk in it, and Gautham cried silently in agony with every sip that he took. It almost felt as though his grandfather was right beside him at that moment. Perhaps he too was sipping his cup of cardamom tea at that very moment somewhere. Perhaps there was a tea shop in heaven too. Smiling slightly, Gautham began walking again, gesturing to his friends to follow him. He climbed down the stairs into the underground tunnel, the one which connected the new campus to the old campus. One of the many street dogs that lurked around began to follow him, as it usually did. Another dog, another memory. His grandfather had told him of his childhood when he had owned a dog called Bhairav. Taatha had loved that dog with all his heart, playing with him all the time and taking care of him. He had told Gautham how the death of that dog had created a huge void in his young life. He had been twelve when Bhairav died. Seeing death so closely at that age had shaken him up, but it had also made him understand the temporariness of life. It had prepared him to understand the impact that the death of a loved one has on a person. It might have been a dog that had died, but the love was no less than any other. Years later, his grandfather had seen the death of his twenty-year-old son in a motorbike accident. Gautham's mother always recalled how composed her father had been after that incident. He had shed tears and grieved, yes, but he had also accepted his son's death faster than any of the other family members had. Gautham now wished he had learnt how to accept death as well. It was painful that his grandfather's death was the one to give him that first taste of the feeling of separation.

As they were about to enter Dorm 24, Gautham saw the volleyball team practising in the court outside the dorm. Volleyball, the sport of able people! That is what his grandfather used to call the sport. He had hated cricket. According to him, it was the laziest sport on the planet. He had been a volleyball player himself and had taught Gautham to play the game as well.

The ball rolled towards Gautham's feet now. One of the players had attempted a block and failed. Gautham picked up the ball and threw it towards the other side of the court. It was a good throw. But his grandfather would have probably criticised it. He hadn't timed the shot well. The man had always wanted perfection when it came to volleyball, unlike mathematics. Ah! The old hypocrite.

Gautham waved to the player nearest to him and asked if he could get another chance to serve the ball. Once again, his friends could not hide their bemusement and shock. The volleyball team obliged him, hesitantly so. He threw the ball up and looked at the night sky. Between the halos of the court lights, he saw an old man smiling gently at him. And it was not just any old man. It was *his* old man. Gautham jumped, leaving a flying tear behind. He could no longer see the ball; it was only the old man's white beard that he focussed on. His hand connected with the ball and it whizzed into the other side of the court. The old man smiled, this time with pride. Gautham landed back softly. His tear seemed to have waited for him at the very location where he had left it a second ago. He smiled, and with a small nod to no one in particular, he resumed walking back to his dorm.

The minute he opened the door to his room, Neeta got busy. She picked up an empty duffel bag from under his bed and began filling it with some clothes and essentials. Abhishek walked over to his desk and logged into his laptop to book the flight ticket. As Gautham looked around his room, his eyes fell on the sandalwood idol of Lord Krishna kept on a shelf in a corner. His grandfather's last gift to him, as had been his first, was an idol of the God he had loved most. He picked up the brown figurine lovingly and not reverently. He did not see Krishna in it anymore, but only the touch of his grandfather.

"Will you be able to make it for the 10:15 pm flight? It's almost 8:30 pm now," Abhishek asked.

"Of course he can," Neeta replied, stuffing his bag with the casemat of Financial Markets, which was the first exam, while making sure that no one saw her do that.

"Okay. Am booking it then."

"Wait! Don't!" Gautham spoke out, the words coming out of his mouth almost involuntarily.

"Huh? But why not, Gauti?"

"Umm . . ." Gautham faltered. "Ugh . . . I don't think I want to go. I don't think I need to."

"What? You said . . ."

"I know. I know. But I don't think my grandfather would have wanted me to come anyway. He always prioritised my studies over everything else."

"But he is no longer . . ."

"Yes. But I don't think it would have mattered to him anyway . . ."

After another forty minutes of trying to explain things to them, his friends left his room. Gautham sank back into his bed. He knew why he did not feel the need to go home anymore. His grandfather had not really left him. He was here, there, and just about everywhere. Just like Krishna. His Taatha was within him. When he had had a vision of him at the volleyball court, that's when Gautham had understood this. He knew why he had been able to see that vision. It was perhaps his grandfather's way of telling him to accept what had happened. Perhaps he was telling him that his life at IIMA was not so hectic and cruel after all. It was simply what it was. He had to take it as he saw it. His grandfather was there, in every corner of the red-bricked campus. He just had to learn to see that and accept it. That cup of cardamom tea and those dogs that followed him around, they were there to remind him of this truth. Gautham closed his eyes. He saw his grandfather smiling that charming, infectious smile of his. That one image played repeatedly inside his head now, as if it was on loop. He laughed along with his grandfather now. They laughed together. It was bliss. It was his childhood all over again. It was not painful. Not anymore.

He opened his eyes a little while later. And then he opened his marketing casemat. The last drop of tear blotted some of the text on the page that lay open on the table. But he did not care anymore. It was 9:50 pm. He had closed the last door to Chennai. Rather, his grandfather had. He had moved on. And it was time for him to do the same.

Mr Peace in PGP2

SIDDHARTHA BHASKER

∽∞∽

Peace, our protagonist for this story, wakes up at 7:00 am. After his daily morning chores, he takes a bath and sits for puja. His neighbour, Loadu, knocks on his door just then.

"Want to smoke a cigarette?" Loadu asks, smiling at him.

"No. You know I have quit and I hate to smoke now. Still, you come in every day at exactly this time and interfere in my puja!"

"Oh ho! Sorry, Peace. Won't happen again."

"Better never."

"I am so stressed over the presentation today, man. What if the professor just screws me in front of the whole class?"

"Nothing wrong in getting screwed by the professor. That's the whole idea of these presentations."

"I cannot believe you are so cool and collected. I am shitting in my pants here just thinking about all the questions he is probably going to ask me. I just want to run away from this place!"

"Go and fret in your room, Loadu. I am doing puja."

Incense stick in hand, Peace squats on a saffron-coloured mat in front of the small pantheon of gods in his room—Hanuman, Shiv, and Saraswati. Sanskrit *shlokas* (verses) effortlessly flow out from his mouth as he offers his reverence to the deities. He prays for the good health of his loved ones and for peace in the world.

He has his breakfast in the mess at 8:15 am and reaches Class Room 4 at 8:40 am. He takes the front row seat and once the lectures begin, he takes notes scrupulously. After the two morning classes, he goes to the library to revise the day's learnings and to complete the assignments. At two, he has his lunch in the mess, after which he sleeps for an hour. The alarm wakes him up at 3:45 pm. He has two more classes to attend in the evening.

In the first class, he has to present as part of a group. He stands confidently at the centre of the well, the focal place in the class from where the professor teaches, and leads his group mates through the presentation. Much to the amazement of everyone present, he answers every question that's thrown at him and the presentation is so good that everybody, including the professor, claps at the end. In the second class, he raises his hand to answer each and every question the professor asks, but somehow, his turn never comes. Finally, his persistence pays off when the professor asks him gently, "Mr Peace, tell me, what is your goal in life?"

He hadn't expected this. He isn't prepared for this. He freezes. His heart rate fastens and tension grips his body. Everybody is looking at him, expecting an answer. He sees Loadu sitting in the last row, laughing silently. He is sweating. Profusely.

"*Nahiiiii*!!!"

He wakes up suddenly with a jerk. His eyes go straight to the twirling fan overhead.

"Not again, man," he says to himself, looking around his dorm room. This is not the first time he has had the dream. The clock on his table tells him it's 2:00 pm. He checks whether he had set an alarm the previous night before sleeping. He hadn't. He has missed all his classes for the day.

He gets up, goes out, and knocks on his neighbour's door.

"*Sutta hai kya?* Got a cigarette?"

Loadu glares at him.

"*Besharam kahin ka.* So shameless, always asking for a cigarette! Today, the professor was asking about you. Your attendance is going to fall short. Debar *kar denge tujhe.* They'll debar you."

"*Karne de yaar. Jab karenge tab dekha jayega.* Let them do it. I'll deal with it when they actually debar me. Now, hand me a *sutta*," Peace snaps back. He notices a cigarette packet kept on Loadu's table and picks up one cigarette.

Next, he places an order from Bizarre, an eating joint on the campus, and then goes to the bathroom where he spends around 30 minutes dreaming. He dreams of the casinos of Las Vegas where he might get posted if he got into the company of his choice. He dreams of the women of Russia, a country he plans to definitely visit sometime within the next few years. He also dreams about getting an A in at least one course in his MBA programmme. He has had to be content with Bs and Cs as of now. When the food gets delivered, he eats quickly and remembers only midway through the meal that he has forgotten to brush, which he does later, as soon as he finishes the meal. He gets a call from his friend a little after that.

"Movie *dekhni hai?* Want to watch a movie? *Ek* ticket available *hai.* I've got one spare ticket."

"*Paise nahi hain.* I don't have any money."

"*Koi nahi. Aaja.* Come anyway. The show's in half an hour."

The movie is an art movie. Peace sits through the whole thing, staring at the screen blankly. He tries to go deep into the movie like some of the art commentators, sifting through things like the logical consistency in the story, the shades of lighting, the camera work, the character sketches, etc. But he gives up after a while and allows his thoughts to run away towards the bright glittering lights of the casinos of Las Vegas.

After the movie, he spends half an hour at Ram Bhai's, talking to his sutta friends about the job scene. Peace wants a Pre-Placement Offer (PPO) from the company he had interned for. But it looks highly unlikely after his performance during the internship. On the last day of the internship, his boss, who was fed up with him, politely asked him to change his ways if he wanted to survive in the corporate world in the future. Peace had nodded his head, only half listening to the man go on and on. He had been happy that he was getting back to his life on campus. Walking back from Ram Bhai's, he then sits for an hour at the LKP with his section mates, playing Criminal. He loves the game and can play it for hours. He loses many times, but he does not mind it. The fun is in the playing and the accompanying commentary, not in the winning. His mobile rings just as they finish a game.

"Peace, we are meeting at 11 pm in Pinki's room to work on the presentation." It is one of his study group mates on the line.

"Yeah, okay. I'll be there."

He has dinner with one of his co-interns at Bizarre, where he meets his poker friends.

"We start at 11 pm, Peace," one of them reminds him.

"Yep! I'll be there!" Peace replies.

After dinner, Peace comes back to his room and sits down to play Age of Empires. At 11 pm, he gets two consecutive calls. One is from his study group mates and the other is from his poker friends. He misses one of them and picks up the other.

Poker goes on the whole night. The stakes became higher. And higher. After a while, Peace goes all-in. He stays there for the whole duration of the game, until the game is finally up and everyone goes back to their rooms.

At 5 in the morning, Peace sits down to enjoy his Maggi at Suresh Bhai's Nescafé stall. Suresh Bhai has become his best friend over time. His shop is open twenty-four hours a day and Peace visits him almost daily. With a wide grin and a quick pat on his back for every self-made joke that Peace cracks, Suresh Bhai always adds an extra packet of masala to Peace's Maggi. Peace would generally stay back long after he finishes eating the Maggi to talk to Suresh Bhai and tell him about his day and the classes he has missed.

"Are you going to the Public Finance class tomorrow?" a batchmate who has come out for a glass of cold coffee asks him.

"Yeah," Peace says, nodding his head and twirling the white plastic fork around the last of his Maggi. "It is at 10:20 am, right? I will set an alarm today before sleeping."

An hour or so later, Peace walks into his room to find a dog sitting on his bed. The dog quietly looks at him. Peace sits on his bed and the dog shifts closer, eventually curling up in his arms. When the dog starts licking him, Peace gets a little irritated. After shooing it out of his room, he changes his bedsheet, switches off the lights, downloads a movie, and starts watching it on his laptop. It is a crime drama, his favourite genre. Eventually, Mr Peace drifts off to sleep, the movie continuing to play on his laptop, its heavy background score keeping his dreams company. It is 7 am.

Four Walls Don't Make a Classroom

YATIN KAMAT

⁂

On a warm October morning, I found myself sitting in a classroom in IIMA and staring into an abyss, having given up on trying to make sense of the concepts that the microeconomics professor was teaching with an air of nonchalance. My eyes swept across the classroom and I noticed mixed expressions on the faces of all the students present. As the professor sketched away formulae and graphs on the blackboard, some of my batchmates, the 'brightest minds in the country', gaped at the blackboard with furrowed eyebrows, each one of them waiting for their moment of epiphany, when there would be that slight nod of the head and that subtle glint of understanding that would creep into their eyes. Some got to that moment quicker than the others, while some sat through the class with the same stoic expression on their faces. There were those who furiously—albeit, a tad mindlessly—scribbled in their notebooks as the class went on. Their eyes would go to the board and then come back to their notebooks where they would note down every comma and curve the professor drew on the board, much like a painter looking up from his easel at his subject and then painting it as it is. The only voice in the class was the heavy and clear voice of the professor who was passing through the graphs of consumer theory like one would pass over the scenes of a well-made movie, the current scene leading sublimely to the next, creating an elegant story. Not everyone in the class was interested though.

The couple in the upper right corner of the classroom, for instance, seemed to be too caught up with enjoying their honeymoon phase—that beautiful time when the lovebirds are still getting to know each other, the playful banter helping them mask the pain of academic drudgery—to care about anything else. The girl nudged the boy after the professor made a particularly convoluted remark about consumer theory, and the boy wrote something in her notebook. She read it. And they giggled. She kept stealing discreet glances at the professor to check if they were attracting his unwanted attention. Thankfully, he did not care either.

Quite a few of the boys seemed to have their hands hidden below their desks, staring at their crotches and smiling intently. Hopefully, they were only using their mobile phones and not doing anything else. Some of them had lost all interest. They never even looked at the blackboard. Their disinterest, however, could not be taken as a weakness. Far from it. They had all networked well and were probably sure about getting all the notes, which they would then read just before the exams to get through. Understanding the concepts being taught in class was not their priority.

As the professor went on with his lecture, I peeked into the notebook of the guy sitting on my right. We weren't friends really, he was just my neighbour in class. What we did have in common though was our complete lack of interest in the squiggles the professor was drawing to explain what 'indifference curves' were. As the man droned on, my neighbour sketched away in his notebook. It was a lovely sunset scene and I couldn't help commenting, "You're really good at this. You should sketch more often."

He laughed it off. "I'm not that good, my friend. I'm just an amateur."

"Maybe, but you do have an artist in you."

"Hmm . . . on that note, I have noticed that you spend most lectures scribbling poems and stories in your notebook. And from whatever I've managed to read so far, it's really good! You should consider writing a blog or maybe publishing some of the stories."

"Ha!" I scoffed. "I don't think so, man. I only write to pass time."

He shrugged and got back to his sketching while I continued to write my story and think about why we sometimes need people to believe in us before we start believing in ourselves, and why lightning has to strike before a thunderstorm hits. Just then, a lively discussion gripped the class, breaking my train of (unrelated) thoughts. Someone had mentioned the recent buyout of an Indian firm by a foreign corporate behemoth, and several hands had shot up in anticipation of an opportunity to speak and score some points with the professor. The professor gave them a chance one by one. I listened to the first student out of curiosity. The girl was trying to connect what the professor had just taught to the repercussions of the buyout, but it was a rather random and tenuous connection, as if she was throwing a dart blindfolded.

I turned to my neighbour and we started chatting again. Before too long, however, the guy sitting behind me snapped at us, "What's being taught is critical. So could the two of you please shut up and let me listen to what the professor has to say?"

Amused and a little embarrassed to have been caught in the wrong, we got back to our own avocations and let the future governor of the RBI resume the pursuit of his ambitions.

As I pushed my seat back in an effort to relax, I wondered if the prominent cricket commentator, the RBI governor, and the popular-yet-controversial Indian author, all alumni of this formidable institution, had sat in these very classrooms and ever worried about whether they'd end up doing the things they really wanted to do or not? Had they been like the friends I often saw gazing at the blackboard with the concentration of a mystic or had they been like me and my neighbour? Pursuing their heartfelt passions while entangled in the trap of their ambitions? Had they raised their hands with zillions of doubts yet to be solved or had their heads been lowered into the storybooks they had brought to class to pass time? I yearned to know what they must have been like. But there was no way I could find out.

I tried to refocus on the lecture, but yet again, I was distracted. This time by the girl sitting two rows in front of me in the well. The first time I had seen her, I remember telling myself that she looked really pretty. It had been hard to miss her in that class of strangers. Now, as I stared at her from behind, she tossed her hair back several times and I wondered how many of us in that room skipped a heartbeat every time she did that.

Boy, was she a sight for sore eyes! Dressed casually in a top and a pair of jeans, she probably didn't want to make a statement, but she had, unknowingly so, ended up carving out a magical space for herself within these red brick walls. I took a deep breath in and let out a silent 'wow'.

When the clock finally signalled that it was 1:10 pm, the professor wrapped up his session and everybody shuffled out hastily to leave for lunch.

In that moment, as I continued to sit in my seat, I thought to myself, "While they ended up venturing down different paths—the governor, the author, and the commentator—they all laid the foundations of their dreams right here. And incidentally, each one of them met the love of their lives in these very classrooms!"

As the class emptied out, I found myself moving towards the front of the class where that potential 'special someone' sat gathering her books and notebooks.

"Hey!" I said when I was right behind her. She turned around and looked up at me enquiringly. "Umm . . . There's this WAC assignment coming up that's to be done in pairs. Would you like to do it with me?"

She tossed her hair yet again, and stuffing her books into her bag, she smiled at me and said, "Yes, why not!"

"Great. I'll . . . umm . . ." I faltered, taken aback by her quick acceptance. "I'll see you soon then." I stood there, fidgeting a little. "Would you, would you like to have coffee with me? In the cafeteria?"

She looked at me with surprise. Then a faint smile glowed through her lips. "Now?"

"Yeah, if you are free."

"Sure!" she said, zipping her bag close and standing up.

I picked up my notebook with the unfinished story inside it and left the classroom with her. As she talked about the class and the professor, I thought about what exactly it was that I was getting from this class. What was the utility, as the professor would have put it, of sitting there in the classroom for the whole duration of the lecture? Could I have achieved greater utility in that same duration of time by doing something else? And then it occurred to me.

Four walls don't make a classroom. A classroom is a reflection of the people inside it and of their dreams. Some dream of fulfilling their ambitions. And some dream of finding happiness.

Four walls don't make a classroom. A classroom is made of all the stories that exist within it. And I wonder now, where this one story truly belongs—inside this book or within that classroom?

Reunion

NIKITA BHARADIA

∽∞∽

The roads of Ahmedabad were full that day. People were crossing each other in such a hurried fashion that it could only be justified by a zombie outbreak. Looking out through the dusty windshield of the cab, Aranya could smell the dampness in the weather and the stagnancy which marked the not-so-upbeat life of Ahmedabad. As the green signboard heralded the arrival of her college, her heart started thumping loudly. She was visiting her alma mater after five years and she was quite nervous, as one is wont to be when meeting someone after the last goodbye, expecting them to be frozen in time with a part of you from long ago. She uttered the words "Dorm 2, Room 34," unconsciously, under her breath. Some things get etched deep in one's memory and they come pouring out at the slightest of stirrings. And this trip back to Ahmedabad was more than just a slight stir.

The cab dropped her at the gate. She got out, picked up her luggage, paid the driver, and started walking into the darkness that would unleash the lush green heart of this sacred institution—the Louis Kahn Plaza.

When she got to the Plaza, she stationed herself at the edge of the vast green expanse, steeling herself against the inevitable assault of a hundred different memories. She stood there, waiting for someone very special. A man, a boy rather, for she had met him as a student in her first year here. Shy yet ambitious, and with an addiction for tea, something about him had instantly put her at ease and they had become friends in that first year itself. They had spent a considerable amount of time together, choosing the same courses and working on assignments together. And as things turned out, they had gradually transitioned into being more than just friends. They had held hands while walking alongside the LKP on numerous occasions in that distant past. They had kissed furtively in his room and made out a couple of times as well. Life had been a bed of roses then. Eventually though, they had passed out of the institute and gone to work in separate cities, having bagged lucrative job offers during campus placements. And somehow, in the humdrum patterns of their new hectic lives, they had lost touch with each other. Over time, the distances widened so much that it looked like they had forgotten all about the times they had spent together. Or had they?

Before she could push back at these thoughts and return to her present reality, she felt a touch on her shoulder. She turned around. It was him. The same as before, standing tall and straight with his hands in his pockets, and staring at her with his typical not-too-big and not-too-small smile. When had she seen him last? Two years ago? Or was it three? But here they were; destiny had brought them back together to the very place where their story had begun all those years ago.

She started the conversation by commenting on his looks and the fake accent he appeared to have acquired during his last global stint and invited a counter remark on her supposedly haughty attitude. A few laughs, a few glances stolen from the corner of their eyes, and the spark of his hand touching her fingers casually . . . She remembered his lips caressing hers on the last night they had spent together before they left for their respective jobs. She remembered the words that had been spoken, the promises that had been made in that darkened dorm room. He never spoke about it. She never uttered the words that would concretise their existence either.

As the sunlight mellowed, so did their inhibitions around each other. Starting from awkward and slightly stilted conversations about their work, they began delving into the details of their mundane lives, the daily anecdotes that mark each day, and the ups and downs that came their way. Hours flew by. Shadows started lengthening and birds started retreating to their nests. Night, when it came, crept in silently, without them noticing it. He mentioned his wife in passing, and she could decipher from the woman's name that she was French. She wanted to know more about her, about whether he was in love with her or not, and she with him. She wanted to know whether he had children who witnessed the love of their parents or not. And she wanted to hear him say that he had never forgotten her. But he never gave her a hint about what went on in his heart. His personal life was out of bounds.

The institute had arranged for an alumni dinner. Their batchmates, who had come from all over the world, were moving towards the new campus lawns where the dinner spread had been laid out. The two of them watched them walk past the Plaza. They should have gotten up and joined them for the alumni dinner as well. After all, that dinner was the whole reason why they were all there. But the moonlight was too beautiful and the time they had with each other was too sacred for them to allow the others to intrude in. They wanted all this time for themselves. It was as if they were young again and couldn't care less about the world beyond. Some of their batchmates passed a remark or two as they crossed the two of them sitting right in the middle of the lawn. But the remarks were always greeted with a smile. The others probably knew what they were feeling. So, they let them be.

She wondered how she could talk to him so much without thinking! How time flew like a breeze when they were together! How life felt young, like a lovely summer on the beaches of Europe! How they filled each other with passion! Did she still love him? After all this time?Or was it her imagination? Who could define what love was? True, she had someone else in her life now, but this man from her past, sitting beside her and talking the night away, his presence was always there somewhere in the recesses of her mind.

She turned and looked at him. There he sat with a cup of tea in his hand. And there was her heart. Beating hard again. Skipping a beat. Somersaulting. Heady with his nearness. Didn't this love break the rules of society, casting her as a moral outlaw? A little bolt of anger shot through her blood. For being so naive. For being so careless about things. But how could she be angry for taking away something that was never with her in the first place?!

She wanted time to be just another page in her book so that she could tear it off and rewrite their story. When she had foolishly believed that it was time that was at her mercy and not the other way round, she used to define love in parameters. Love was always about balance. A balance between the heart, mind, and body. They had found that balance when they had been students. But then they had lost it somehow. Didn't that mean that their love had never been pure to begin with?

Hence, ignoring every pulse and every thought that had screamed the opposite, she had never accepted that she loved him. Why would she? Love, she knew, would have eventually fallen apart, breaking the very friendship that had caused it to bloom in the first place. She had left people behind in the past and she was not ready to face another head-on collision again. It was, she had decided, a feeling best left unexplored. Theirs was a bond that shouldn't have grown deeper.

They both had accepted what had been left unsaid. It was something that would always be there, lingering between them. After all, not every love lasts a lifetime. Not every love is defined and not every love requires owning the other person. She had been told that love was a 'one person for a lifetime' affair. But as she experienced it in her life, it showed up in parts. Some people found love in scattered moments, some grew old and died in the arms of their first loves, and some people left behind their loves, only to have them follow them like a shadow. Only if they could throw away all those movies and books which decreed the love theory, the world would have been a more bearable place.

The two of them stood up eventually and decided to take a stroll through the corridors, just like the old times. Walking through those long lonely corridors, she found that her hands were trembling. The dilemmas in her heart were beginning to become a little overwhelming. He touched her fingers. Gently. She didn't know if it was deliberate or accidental. He was talking about taking early retirement and settling in the hills where he had bought a villa. He threw away the teacup in his hand into a dustbin and then took out his handkerchief to clean his hands. When he kept the handkerchief back in his pockets and let his hands fall to his sides, she slowly slid her fingers through his. He didn't stop talking. He didn't stop mid-stride. He didn't question her motives. He simply let it happen. He held her hand a little tighter and walked. He was inviting her to his place in the hills, telling her about the apple trees in the garden under which she could tie a hammock and while time away.

She nodded her head. The tomorrow that he was talking about, it would be another race against the tricks that life played, but tonight was only theirs, with no one and nothing to hold them back.

Angel of Love

RAJIV RANJAN

∽∞∽

It was around 5:40 pm and the social entrepreneurship class for the second year (PGP2) students had just ended. The atmosphere inside the classroom, however, seemed a bit unusual because the students, instead of rushing back to their respective dorms, were busy talking about the story they had just heard. The guest speaker in their class that day had been a woman named Manan. Tall, thin, dark-skinned, and with an angular face, she was about fifteen years senior to them and had talked for an hour about her initiatives, her struggles, and the fruits of her hard labour.

Fresh out of the National Institute of Fashion Technology (NIFT), Delhi, the best institute in the field in the country, she had obtained a scholarship for the International Fashion Academy in Paris and was planning to pursue an MBA in Fashion Business there. She was in the purple patch of her life. She wanted to design the most stylish and expensive clothes ever. She wanted to walk up the international ramps in style, leading the fashion parades. She wanted to be famous and rich and glamorous like the icons she adored. But was life planning the same for her? No. Definitely not. For as it does in most cases, life had a very different trick hidden up its sleeve for Manan.

What happened on the chilly night of 21 December 1998 which changed the course of Manan's life so dramatically? Why did Manan decide to pursue a completely different path from the one she had always dreamt of? What was it that struck her so deeply that she decided to throw away her childhood dreams in a heartbeat? In the one hour that Manan spent with the PGP2 students, she patiently made her way through many questions like these and allowed the students a glimpse into what her life had been like.

***

Manan was born in a typical Rajasthani bourgeois family in 1977. Her father was a magistrate in Jaipur, and her mother, a homemaker. She grew up a pampered child since she had no siblings and had been born after years of invocations to the gods. From childhood itself, Manan had been good in arts and by the time she was in high school, she had decided that she would become a fashion designer. And in 1994, right after passing her Class 12 board exams, she got selected for the Bachelor's course in Fashion Technology at NIFT, Delhi. This opportunity literally provided wings to her dreams and Manan had a wonderful stint at the institute. By the time she graduated, she had job offers from two multinational corporations and an international scholarship awaiting her consideration.

It would not be wrong to say that some plans are made in heaven, because had Manan not decided to go back to Jaipur to consult her parents regarding her future career plans, things might have unfolded rather differently. She boarded a Jaipur-bound bus on the night of 21 December in a good mood. Images of Europe which she had seen in magazines ran through her mind in a loop. She pictured herself in cold mountain villages, on cushy grasslands, and in serene small towns with beautiful and quaint roadside cafés. As the bus sped away from Delhi, thoughts of a global stint as a super successful fashion designer kept her buoyed. She smiled as she put herself in the shoes of Marina Yee and on the cover of the *Vogue*. She was pretty confident her parents would support her in this endeavour. Life was going to be just wonderful.

Once the bus reached the Sindhi bus stop in Jaipur, she got down and looked for an autorickshaw to ferry her home. As she was walking towards the autorickshaw stand, she saw a little girl, around eleven or twelve years of age, crouched over a scrapheap of trash, searching for whatever discarded pieces of food she could find. The girl was completely naked and had no one else with her. Her hands were frantically removing one piece of waste after the other to find something edible. There were a couple of scraggly dogs around her, sniffing at the trash as she rummaged through it. Manan froze where she was and kept looking. The girl found a half-eaten apple and took it out. She held on to it with one hand and resumed rummaging through the trash for more food. Her stark nakedness and the abject poverty from which she suffered dissolved all the wonderful images of Europe that Manan had conjured up on the bus. Realisation hit her then that while designing clothes for the rich would give her fame and glory and money, it would never put a piece of clothing on the malnourished body of a girl like the one in front of her. Designing clothes was not a profession worth pursuing in a country where people did not have even a scrap of fabric to wear. Manan went home that day and discussed this quandary with her parents who were happy enough to support her changed worldview.

And that's how Manan came to leave her potentially illustrious career as a fashion designer and open a shelter for homeless children, with the first child being that little girl from the bus stand. She named the shelter Surman Sansthan, with the 's' standing for *samanta* (equality), 'u' for *umeed* (hope), 'r' for *raah* (path), 'm' for *mann* (soul), 'a' for *ahaan* (dawn), and 'n' for *nirmal* (pure). Her aim was to incorporate these principles into the very core of the NGO's functioning. Needless to say, it was not an easy journey. Spacial constraints, financial difficulties, and the constant bickering of the elders around her telling her to go back to pursuing her dream of becoming a fashion designer, beset her initial days. And more importantly, Manan had no prior experience of working in an NGO. But through it all, she did not lose hope. Instead, she kept adding to her goals. Over the years, her NGO expanded and grew from one initiative to the next. For instance, through an initiative called Koshish, Manan's NGO now helps widows and homeless women. Through Kyari, the NGO plants trees and helps reduce carbon footprint. And through Jeevan, it helps parents who are in no position to take care of their children's medical conditions. Presently, there are more than a hundred children who Manan provides with food, shelter, clothes, education, and all the other basic necessities of life. Her aim is to make them all capable, provide them with the equality of opportunity they deserve, and make them realise the importance of empathy. She wants to nurture children who can go on to make her dream of India being a poverty-free country a reality. Manan finances her ever-expanding household by selling paintings that she makes herself, by acting in short films, doing stage shows, and running a monthly magazine called *Bougan Vellia*. She has also been bestowed with various accolades over the years for her awe-inspiring contributions to society. Manan dreams of taking her initiative as far as possible.

Even hours after Manan had left them, the students of PGP2 had heated debates about the path she had taken. Some of them found her a little crazy for letting go of an opportunity to study and work in Europe to start an NGO in a small city in India. They were by no means belittling her efforts and her sincerity, but they knew they would never take her path. It was just too unattractive, too far removed from what constituted a good and fulfilling life in their opinion. Some of the students were in awe of her. They found her courageous and inspiring—a true example of what a citizen should be like. Her forsaking a successful career was, in their eyes, an act of selflessness, an act of defiance against social expectations and pressures. They found themselves wanting to do something like what she had done.

Manan's life has been a life of struggle, of idealism, and of compassion. And she chose this life voluntarily, with all her heart. At an age when others race after money, promotions, and illustrious careers, she became a mother to several destitute and homeless children, picking them up from railway platforms, pavements, and even dustbins, legally adopting them and giving them all a chance at living a good life. These children call her "Maa." And quite rightly so. For is she not their mother? Bringing them up with all the love and care a mother gives to her child? Is she not, in the truest sense of the words, an angel of love?

The Deadly Time of 1:45 pm

RAIN WOMAN

There was a picture right at the top of my Facebook timeline—a first-year student standing with an umbrella—and the caption under it read: "Classes cancelled, yippee!!" A million comments were pouring in under this image to congratulate the girl on this extremely unlikely event.

I was in the second year of my PGP course at IIMA. It was that phase in our stint at the institute that was revered as the 'peace time'. Batch after batch of students before me had owned tee shirts that spoke about surviving the first year at IIMA by just thinking about the impending peace of the second year. We could wake up at hours which suited our convenience and were not bound by the demands of a rigorous timetable. We could take up courses which demanded relatively lesser effort from us, and host room and dorm parties all the time. Well, most of us did!

That lazy morning, I had woken up at around 10:15 am to the sound of heavy showers and thunder. A quick look outside showed that it had been pouring all morning. I stepped out of my room to hear music thumping from the basement where most of the first-year students stayed. Someone was playing Sting at a rather loud volume.

"Music at 10:15 in the morning? This is preposterous! Don't they have classes to go to? Is it a mass bunk?!" I thought to myself as I walked up to my neighbour's room. I knocked on her door and pushed it open. My neighbour looked up from her laptop with a frown on her face. "Can you believe it?" she asked, gesturing towards the basement. I wondered if it was a rhetorical question. She continued, "I still have classes to go to while these first-year idiots seem to have gotten the day off! Heavy rains apparently! Why did this never happen to us last year? Huh? Injustice it is, I say!"

At that very moment, another floor mate walked in, visibly drenched and annoyed.

"Damn this campus!!" she cursed. "LKP is flooded. I wanted to go get chai at Ram Bhai's!" She looked a little flustered as she attempted to unlock the door to her room. "Louis Kahn, I tell you, was an overrated architect! Half the campus is flooded, all thanks to him and his crazy ideas! For all you know, CultComm[4] might just announce a parking area pool party!"

Leaving the two of them, I returned to my room. I still had classes to attend at three, after all. Plus, the mood in the dorm was a little too merry for someone whose classes had not been cancelled.

Back in my room, I opened my computer to check my mailbox along with Facebook (again!). The updates kept coming in: "It's a dream come true!"; "No classes today due to heavy rains!" I refreshed my mailbox again. And again. I was still not able to believe that classes had been cancelled. "This is the last thing anyone would've expected in IIMA!" I muttered to myself. In fact, it was the first time in 26 years that classes had been cancelled officially by the PGP office! My bewilderment, in that sense, was very well justified.

However, I lost interest in no time. I had classes to prepare for. I stepped out to the balcony attached to my room, with a cigarette in my hand, thinking, "Ah well! The PGP office does have a heart it seems!" I stood there taking it all in—the pouring rain outside,

---

4   Cultural Committee at IIMA

the music coming from the basement, and the strange festive fervour that appeared to have gripped the entire dorm. I saw a few first-year students walking out of the dorm. They seemed to have dressed up to go out in spite of the rain. I waved at them. "Where are we headed, ladies?" I asked.

"Going out for a movie with the group!" one of the girls shouted back.

Who would have known that a day like this would have been a possibility? That the PGP office had a heart?! Because the odds of them officially cancelling classes were the same as waiting for Karan Johar to make a good art house movie. Or Anurag Kashyap to make one without guns.

A little while later, I went to attend my class. In the first lecture, the professor, quite ironically so, spoke in detail about the water scarcity issues prevalent across India. He talked about Bengaluru and other places in Central India, which had seen a severe depletion in their groundwater levels. Quite a few of my batchmates, who had had a colourful night, were sleeping. I should have tuned off myself, but I found myself asking the professor a question about rains and if a good year of rains would refill the groundwater reserves. I think, in retrospect, it was the weather that made me do it. In response to my question, the professor went into a soliloquy about climate change and how the probability of droughts was going to increase over time, with the wet places getting wetter and the dry ones getting drier.

By the time I got back to my room after the class, the excitement levels in the dorm seemed to have died down. There was no music playing anymore and the dorm seemed empty. I walked up to my neighbour's room.

"Party over already, eh?" I asked, standing at her door and looking in.

She looked up from her laptop and said, "Indeed! Their classes resumed from 11:55 am onwards. Half the junta who had gone out for movies had to leave the theatre and rush back. Sneha is fuming because she had to miss the ending. But who asked them to go out for a movie anyway? Don't they know that things here can change very fast?" A sadistic smile crossed her lips. She looked at me for a moment and then resumed working on the laptop.

"Ah PGP office! You heartless monster!" I thought to myself and walked towards the mess for lunch.

The mess that day was loud and noisy with the first years heatedly discussing the unexpected turns the day had taken so far. Many of them had lost money in advance ticket bookings. When I left the mess after quickly finishing my lunch, the discussions had become mundane and repetitive with everyone angry over the resumption of classes. I had barely walked out of the mess when I saw quite a few students running right past me. They were all headed towards the mess. This mess run could only mean one thing—it was quiz time! There's a very famous saying in Hindi: *Jale par namak chhirakna*, meaning, rubbing salt on one's wound. As the students raced past me, a feeling of vindication ran through my body. After all, one can't really see one's juniors enjoying an entire (rare) day of freedom when one has had to slog it out the whole year. I took out my phone and went to the most faithful source of all news on campus (and even otherwise, I suppose)— Facebook was getting flooded with updates. "Quiz at 2:45 pm, junta!" read one. I checked the time. It was 1:45 pm.

Until last year, I, along with almost all my other batchmates, had dreaded this time of 1:45 pm, for this was when one could get a sudden notification in one's inbox about a quiz being scheduled for any of the first-year courses an hour later. There was never any intimation or hint of what the quiz was actually going to be on. Only wrong guesses!

I turned around and saw the whole bunch of first-year students clambering with their empty plates to get into the lunch line. I knew that there would be others who would skip lunch entirely and would sit somewhere in the campus with their books and notes spread around them, trying to read and remember whatever they could find time for. Every time our batch had a surprise quiz like this coming up, I had always closed myself in my room and read to the best of my ability, my heart beating hard with nervousness.

In no time, the *tuchhas*[5] started updating their Facebook statuses. They were quick to remind the *facchas*[6] that life in the institute was not a bed of roses and that one should be always prepared to take the axe. Their profiles soon became crowded with outbursts of nostalgia, as they fondly remembered the time when they had been the first years. From their words, it almost felt as if they had come out of a gruelling military session successfully. One of them had even put up a picture of the notice board with the quiz notification with a sulky face emoji and had aptly captioned it: "The dark clouds always clear!"

---

5   A term that is used to refer to the second-years students at IIMA.
6   A term that is used to refer to the first-year students at IIMA.

Ixx Globe

ARJUN BHARDWAJ

∽∾∾∽

"*Macha*[7]!" I patted the shoulder of Basudev, the guy sitting in front of me. "Want to bet that the instructor is going to appreciate my insight?"

Basudev had been sleeping with his head perfectly aligned towards the instructor and his eyes open, a skill he had quite an expertise in. He now reacted almost as if he had been woken up in the middle of a nightmare. He looked at me, shrugged his shoulders, and said, "No man! I give up!"

---

[7] Tamil word for brother-in-law; also used as a casual term of reference for a friend

The lecture we were attending was part of a popular course on campus. It went deep, sometimes so deep that Kant and Plato ended up getting roused from their graves. This course required a lot of class participation and most of the students spoke pretty confidently about their opinions in class. Actually, that was the case with most of us, in most of our classes. If anything, when we spoke in class, it was in a voice of great confidence. This was a skill so neatly and quickly acquired by everyone at IIMA that it became a part of our personalities pretty soon. This skill set was popularly known across the campus as 'globe'.

For those who are unaware of what 'globe' stands for in this context, it is essentially the ability to talk about anything under the sun without really knowing anything about it. One day you could be Bill Gates propagating ideas for global healthcare, and on another day you could be an Indian farmer talking about the failure of monsoons and recurring agrarian debt. You could be a feminist talking about gender equality and the glass ceiling in the corporate world, or you could be a business tycoon who has succeeded despite the unfavourable investment environment of the country. All of this, without having any real experience of being these people. This ability to talk is a skill that all MBA students acquire almost without any effort. It's the recipe for success for many in their lives ahead. All it takes is a heaped spoonful of jargon, a handful of animated gesticulations, and a generous dollop of "it depends!" after every couple of lines. That's it!

There is a rich plethora of globes on the offer. There is the normal harmless globe where you are trying to escape from the clutches of a professor who cold-called you just when you were about to drift off into a blissful stupor. Then there is the ultra-globe, which is the arbitrary globe that you use when you realise that you are going to fail in the class participation component of the course. The kill-me-now-globe is where you look with wonder at the person who perpetrated such an atrocity upon his classmates and the professor present by speaking of non-existent things or connections, forcing you to start questioning said person's mental acumen.

In this assortment of globes, the one kind which has no match is the Ixx globe. Ixx, which stands for Information xx (last part of the course name has been changed for obvious reasons!), was a course taken by a professor whose teaching style was a bit of an acquired taste, to be honest. His idea of a class was to open up a blank presentation, just throw a question at the class, and then leave the house open for participation. And everyone had to participate as the hawk-like gaze of the teaching assistant kept us all alert. The points the students presented were noted down onto the presentation till the end of the class. The professor made sure every point had been debated and then weaved a concluding narrative covering the entire discussion. Of course, a class like that also provided a rather conducive environment for students practicing their globing skills.

I had been a fairly reserved student till then, refraining from globing unless it was absolutely required. I came from an engineering background and globing didn't come naturally to me. In engineering courses, there are perfectly correct answers. You either know them or you don't. In this course, however, that wasn't quite the case. It was difficult for me to shed my engineering habits. But some classes urge you to globe. They provide constant provocation, much like those mouth-watering sweets which everyone wants to have. Almost everyone had shown their globing skills in this particular class and with every passing week, I felt the professor's expectant gaze landing on me every now and then, as if hoping that someday my mouth would open up and I, too, would become a part of this tradition of globing. But that didn't happen. Well, not until the day when after a sleepless night of parties and mindless fun, I hopped into class with a sense of buoyant hope and destiny. The professor came in a little later, at around 8:45 am, and as he opened up his usual blank presentation, he asked us, "What is knowledge?"

The answers began to pour in one after the other, most of them making almost everyone in the class cringe. "Knowledge is the accumulation of facts," said a student, looking at the teaching assistant throughout to see if she had heard him. "Knowledge is more than an accumulation of facts; it's establishing a connection between them, like connecting all the dots," said another one who I knew had brought a novel along to read discreetly if things got too boring. "Knowledge has got nothing to do with facts. It's an understanding of the nature of the world," shouted a student who was quite the pro at globing. "There can be no understanding of the world without relevant facts! Facts are a subset of knowledge," pointed out another one.

This went on for about 30 minutes, after which there was a silence, for people had finally run out of things to say. Then our class representative, who had just woken up from his deep slumber, said, "Knowledge is an asset."

Now I had been barely tolerating everyone's random globing till then, but at the class rep's answer, something broke inside me, and the normally morose me rudely cut short another poor soul trying to garner some class participation marks and shouted, "Knowledge is a liability!" A half a second of silence, and then raucous laughter greeted my answer. The professor asked me to explain.

"Sir," I said, looking at him, "knowledge is a long-term asset and a short-term liability. If I know something, then that bit of knowledge stays with me for a long time, at least in my subconscious it does, and hence it's a long-term asset. However, if what I know is something controversial or something that's likely to harm someone, say for instance I somehow come to know that you are going to be murdered, then I am under the liability to tell you about it. So then this piece of knowledge becomes a short-term liability!" I sat back in my chair, pretty darn sure that my Financial Accounting professor would have been proud of me had he seen me globe.

The professor waited for someone from the class to pitch in with their own version of globe. But the class was silent. I watched with trepidation as the professor tapped the marker on his desk. Then, he turned around and wrote down the point I had just made on the board. He turned back to face me and for a second I felt my throat go dry. Would he rip me apart? But his response was a resounding positive: "Excellent insight!"

I had done it! I had now been initiated into the globing tradition in his course! I thought that I might just have produced the best globe ever in this course. A sense of pride filled me. I was smiling as I kept looking at my point scribbled on the green board with white chalk, while the class moved on to other discussions.

Presenting Ravana

K CHANDRASEKARAN

~~~

When you enter your second year at IIMA as a valiant survivor, a tuchcha, you are in for a memorable year that will be spent high on 'spirits'. PGP2 is when you have the time to 'weed' out the unnecessary elements and focus on what interests you: music, marketing, finance, movies, or just about anything. In sharp contrast to the first year at the institute, the second year can be a truly relaxing experience if one chooses the right courses.

Our friend—let's call him Ravana, shall we?—was a popular member of the campus basketball team, and he felt that he was right on track to live out the second year in peace, having secured a Pre-Placement Offer already. It would be a throwback to his final year in undergraduation, he thought. He had chosen what were known as the best 'chill' courses according to his peers. And they had, so far, lived up to that label. All except one course, where the professor had formed random groups for the purpose of a class presentation. But Ravana, who had burnt a special kind of grass all night, was in a parallel world and didn't care a whit about what was going on in the class.

Groups, as any MBA student would know, are the heart of a course. You can't pass a course if your group is not working well as a unit. Many courses rely heavily on group presentations and group assignments, so much so that the performance of the group as a whole could make or break your chances of passing the course. The camaraderie between the group members, therefore, becomes a key factor in achieving all the deliverables for a course. More often than not, most group members find the time and sit together, for hours on end, to finish the requirements. If there is a presentation to be made, they decide their roles on the spot, during the presentation. Each one takes a different part of the presentation to read and present. The working of a group is supposed to be like that of well-oiled machinery, with each component feeding into another to bring out a quality product.

Unfortunately, however, every group does not work this way.

Every student who has sat through even a basic economics course knows about something called the free-rider problem. Free riders are those agents who put in little to no effort in group activities but are beaming recipients of the group's fruits of labour. Free riders spoil the mood of other group members. They receive the fruits, along with the curses (silent ones mostly) as well. Here too, there were a number of free riders who knew that their group members would do all the work because they cared too much about their marks to leave things in someone else's control. Ravana was one among them.

He was daydreaming in class when the groups were being announced. The previous night's party had resulted in a glorious hangover. The names the professor was calling out crossed his mind like cars in full speed pass a tottering drunk man at the edge of a road. Group after group had been announced and his name was yet to come. Or had he missed it? No, he heard it now: Rajnikanth, Group 8. Yes, yes, Rajnikanth is his first name.

As the course progressed and other groups presented their analyses, Ravana patiently waited for a chance to present with his group so as to get done with the class participation component of the course. Then one fine day, the professor announced, "Group 8, tomorrow is your presentation. Please come prepared." This was it, Ravana told himself. He had to work on this presentation and just finish it off. He could then relax and afford to bunk a few more classes.

Ravana planned out the remainder of his day meticulously. A couple of hours of basketball, then read the case, prepare the analyses, and surprise his group members with the PPT. His dorm mates were putting on a 'session' that night and he could not afford to miss it. So he would have to work real fast on the PPT. That wouldn't be a problem, he knew he could crack it quickly enough if he put his mind to it.

A little later, on his way back from the basketball court, Ravana stopped at CT to order a nutritious health drink, for he had spent a lot of energy on the game of basketball. He was waiting at the counter for the drink when he turned and looked around the place. At one of the tables near the counter, a familiar figure from the same course was busy working on the case meant for Ravana's group presentation the next day. Connecting the dots, he approached the girl and with the familiarity of a group member, he looked down at her with a wide grin on his face and enquired, "Hey! How's the PPT coming along?"

Ravana was known across his batch as a free rider. Therefore, when the girl looked up from her work, surprised at Ravana's enquiry, and replied, "Yeah . . . umm . . . I am almost done with it," it wasn't really all that surprising.

"Oh great! Tell me if you need any help!" offered Ravana, and collecting his health drink, he left CT, giving a hearty thumbs-up to the girl on his way out. Mentally, he struck off one item from his checklist as he walked out. He now just had to read the case and then it was time to PARTYYYYYY!

Later in the day, Ravana forgot all about the case and the fact that he was supposed to read it. Instead, he partied. Hard. The next morning, he went to the class extremely tired and sleepy, and slumped into one of the seats in the upper deck, as far away from the professor's line of sight as he could manage. As usual, Ravana was unable to concentrate on the lecture the professor was delivering and despite his valiant attempts to stay conscious, he was soon napping. Sometimes, luck turns the bad way. He was chasing the proverbial rabbit when he felt somebody prodding him in the back. Reluctantly rousing himself, he shifted slightly in his seat and realised that it was his neighbour. Wordlessly, the guy gestured towards the front of the class. Ravana sat up a little straighter and on realising that everybody in the class was looking at him, he turned towards the professor.

"Yes, sir!" the professor called out, smirking.

"Should I wish you a good evening or a goodnight? Please go and wash your face if you wish to remain in this room."

Ravana hastily got up and walked out of the classroom. While washing his face, he cursed his friend who had recommended this course. It wasn't all that 'chill' a course after all! He returned to the classroom barely five minutes later, only to find his group, Group 8, presenting the case. As Ravana crept in behind the five group members, they all gave him rather strange looks—as if to say, "What the heck are you doing here?"—just like the girl at CT the previous night had. Of course, he was a bit late for the presentation, Ravana told himself, and that explains the looks.

During the rebuttal at the end of the presentation, noticing that his group mates all seemed to be a little ill-prepared for the volley of questions coming their way, Ravana jumped to their rescue. He answered a number of questions with his accumulated knowledge of jargon and globe. It was his five minutes of showing off his hard work and he made the most of it. After they answered the last of the questions, the professor finally let the group go back to their seats.

Making a slight detour on his way back, Ravana approached the Academic Associate (AA) assigned to the course and asked, "You saw me speak, right? So my presentation component is counted?"

"Yeah, I saw you up there," the woman replied. "What's your name?"

"Ravana, ma'am. Rajnikanth Ravana."

"Ummm . . ." The woman ran a finger down a list of names before looking up at Ravana with a quizzical expression on her face. "There is a Rajnikanth in Group 8, but not a Rajnikanth Ravana. Are you sure this is your group?"

The world came crashing down around Ravana. The weird looks that he had gotten from the girl in CT and from all the other group members during the presentation suddenly made sense now. For a second, Ravana imagined all his efforts going to waste, much like a paper boat getting swept away by rainwater in a drain.

"Ma'am, please, please count this as my presentation," Ravana pleaded with the AA now. "I don't know my group number. I must have gotten things confused. It is very much possible that my actual group's presentation is already over. I gave a good presentation today though, didn't I?"

There was a solid slab of tension weighing heavily in the air between them for a few seconds as the AA stared at Ravana. It was almost as if he had asked her out in their very first meeting. But, to his surprise, the sweet AA agreed to his proposal and let him off the hook.

And thus did Ravana pass a course with a 30 per cent presentation weight without much ado. Now he knew he would pass this course. The scenes of a colourful night were already dancing before his eyes as he walked to his seat.

Abhi and Rhea

AJAY KUMAR KATHURIA

Exhausted after the first week of the third trimester, Abhi sat down to take a breather after a long day of lectures and group study. His mind was still on the case report he had to write for the next day's class. He had not expected the workload to be this high at IIMA.

Even as tiredness began to take over, Abhi's mind drifted to what he actually wanted to write about, which was, truth be told, as clichéd a story as they came. He thought about the year he had been through. "We are all slaves of our memories and yet, we go on making more of them," he muttered to his own self. "We can't let go, for we are who we are because of these memories. Many a companies and leaders have failed to survive because they allowed themselves to become victims of their past glories, unable to take decisions based on what the changing times demand . . ."

Abhi decided the assignment could wait. He wanted to write his story: from facing immense pressure and suffering a heartbreak to the exultation of getting the internship he had wanted, it seemed to him that he had seen it all in the first few months itself. Given the insane workload in the first year, he had not given much thought to the events past, with every single day being filled with endlessly long to-do lists and a packed schedule. But there he was, finally getting down to it—writing the case on his life this year past.

About nine months back, he had still been considering whether he should join IIMA or not, and even when he had finally taken the decision to enrol in the institute, he had been unsure about whether it was the right one or not. By late June, however, he was in Ahmedabad and there was just no turning back. Overcoming the apprehensions of being in a new place and with new people, he had found it a little hard to adjust to the unexpected rigours of student life. Eventually, he had settled in and found a group of people he liked hanging out with. But it was Rhea he felt most comfortable with.

That quiet night in September, while sharing a clove-flavoured cigarette with her, he was finally hit by the full force of Rhea's smile. The smile was made more potent by her innocent eyes that embodied a starry night's sparkle in them. Even as she laughed at his poor jokes, he was the one who kept falling for her. Again and again. He was utterly and totally floored. This was a first for him; never had a week-old friendship turned into such a massive one-sided love for him and caught him so off-guard. As clichéd as they come.

As they shared a few more drags of that last cigarette, discussing their hopes, aspirations, goals, and fears, the meandering conversation, which was an end in itself, went on. Eddie Vedder's husky voice in the background lured him into a carefree state and he found himself opening up like never before. Sitting there in the balcony of his room, they lost track of time and it must have been fifteen, twenty minutes, or maybe even more before he realised he had not spoken for a long time.

He was just looking at her, listening intently, smiling and nodding his head every once in a while as an acknowledgement. The music that he could hear was not really there anymore. It was all playing inside his head, the cymbals and the drums and the strings. He was long gone and he knew it. But there was that clichéd twist in their story: the twist of a long-term boyfriend.

The aching tug at his heart was like Christmas—Jingle Bells and Hallelujah! But all the more enchanting—the slight flare of the nostrils when she was angry, the light brown hue of her sun-kissed skin, the ability to talk to each other for hours and eventually knowing what the other was going to say, and sharing that smile. It was his new happy place. Nothing more, nothing less.

It happened at different places, these conversations—his room, her room, a party with a less noisy corner or a nearly empty balcony, the LKP, the sprawling atrium of sorts in the middle of the institute, the original academic building. The sunrise, when caught from the garden surrounding the academic building, looked almost as beautiful as Rhea. And many a sunrise they caught after spending entire nights talking. These conversations were the main draw—the pluck at the strings making wondrous, operatic music. It was as if he was witnessing an artist paint a masterpiece every time he was with Rhea. A masterpiece which imbibed the moments they spent.

The conversations waiting to happen, they stood between them every time they met. It was like waiting for the *Tandava* of peace to begin. The fire of their conversations ready to be lit, ready to be stoked, to be inhaled deep into the lungs for that elusive peace to be brought back to their meandering minds, at once a distraction and a comfort.

The mind digresses. Eventually, he still asked her out; he still took his shot. And failed. The boyfriend was really the fiancé. But persistence is the key, he'd been told. All of this had brought him to this point and he was happier for it. He had come into the institute thinking about a bright and shiny new career, a 360-degree change in his lifestyle, the back-to-school feeling, and the building of a useful network of contacts and allies. He had found most of it—a career direction, an internship, a dramatically different lifestyle, and friends—but most importantly, he had found Rhea.

As he heard a faint sound in the background, Abhi realised the alarm clock had gone off. The clock hands said it was half-past five in the morning. He had not really slept that night, merely rested while his mind busied itself thinking about things past. He sprang to his feet and hit the snooze button. And as in a case, one must take decisions based on the information presented, sometimes allowing for a sprinkle of emotion on top of the layered cake of quantitative analysis. In case analysis, as in real life, Abhi realised that some of his decisions had worked out and some others had not.

The best you can do is to take a call. And in the end, it all comes down to the roll of a dice. The leap of faith just has to be made. And sometimes, fate plays its part too. The fiancé cheats and we call it serendipity. The real case of Abhi and Rhea was not really settled, the decisions had been taken and scenarios had worked out favourably. But the story was just beginning—the dream internship, Mumbai, and then the second year beckoned. Number work, perseverance, and the ability to take decisions, with a little bit of luck thrown into the mix, that's all you really need.

As the clock struck six, Abhi pulled away from his ever-meandering thoughts, realising that the assignment still needed to be completed. Two hours to the deadline, another decision awaited, but one with fewer life-changing consequences.

Time to chop-chop!

Serendipity

SIDDHARTHA BHASKER

One positive externality of studying at IIMA, as far as I was concerned, was my interaction with the women on campus. It may sound vague and strange to most people, but someone like me, who has lived in a small town in a stereotypical middle-class Indian household, would know exactly what I mean. There are innumerable unsaid rules and harsh limits that are imposed on the extent and depth of our social interactions with members of the opposite sex. But in the IIMA campus, a lot of those limits are relaxed, if not being absent altogether, thankfully.

I am neither a 'campus dude' nor a 'full alpha male brimming with testosterone'. What I am is just an average IIMA guy. Someone who has spent a lot of time with books. Someone whose life has been literally devoted to sitting for competitive exams. Someone looking to build a career all his life. The only exception I made was watching movies, foreign ones as well as the regular Bollywood ones available on DC++. I learn from them. In the movies there are parties. And in those parties, guys hit on girls. Whatever may be the ultimate consequence of this, the key thing is my knowledge of 'what to do' and 'what not to do' at parties with girls, and this knowledge is borrowed solely from these movies.

There are lots of awesome parties that happen on the campus: dorm parties, PPO parties, exchange parties, getting-a-job parties, birthday parties, and some strange ones like changing-the-dorm-name party. Some of these parties involve girls, but mostly it's just boys, trippy lights, music, cold drinks, lots of chips, and people high on 'fun'. And to a few of these parties, yours truly is also invited. I am going to narrate to you an incident that occurred during one of the parties held in Dorm 20.

I had managed to see the guest list of the party, so I knew that many of the most well-known faces on the campus were going to be there. The first task for me was to control my urge to go to the party as early as possible. The party was to start at 10 in the night and my itch to get going started at 8:00 pm. At 9:00 pm, I wished someone would just give me a call or knock on my door to ask me to accompany them to the said party. From 10:00 pm to 11:00 pm, I made myself sit on my chair and play Angry Birds. This was not a lesson learnt from a movie but a lesson learnt here, on campus itself: never go to a party on time if you are not close to the host. There will be very few people present, most of them bosom buddies of the host, and inevitably, you will start feeling out of place and that will set the mood for the rest of the night.

Finally, I enter the arena at 11.30 pm. It's important to act cool, to not get excited by the thumping music or the crazy lights. The party has gathered speed. I look out for familiar faces in the crowd and find a few. With the common area of the dorm almost full by now, I shake hands and high-five my way through the crowd to my friends, all of them males. If my eyes meet those of a girl I know and she is considerate enough, she smiles and acknowledges my presence. But I never go over to any of them and none of them take that trouble either.

There is a glass in my hand and the Coke inside it moves as I sway to the music while standing at my place. The music's groovy. People have arranged themselves in loose groups that are constantly seeing an exchange of members. I am standing near the refreshments' table, still contemplating over which group to join. One of the hosts, seeing me standing alone, comes over to share a cigarette. We discuss how good the party is and he tells me about the pains they went through while arranging everything. Then, I suddenly notice a girl waving at me. I don't think I know her, but who cares! I am about to wave back when my host raises his hand. She calls him and gestures that he should join her in a dance. My host nods and starts walking towards her, pulling me along as well. I have been secretly waiting for something like this to happen ever since I had stepped into the party. Hence, I do not offer any resistance.

I start dancing to the song. I have never heard it before, the song I mean. But everybody is so charged up and the excitement is so contagious that it gets to me. When I realise that nobody cares about how badly I dance, it pegs me up further. In a series of original moves, I end up shaking each and every part of my body as if I am getting electrocuted and am trying, desperately so, to get rid of the imaginary live wires I am wrapped up in. This is where I forget the lessons I have learnt from all the movies I have seen: never draw unwanted attention to yourself. Ever. By the time I come to my senses, the circle, of which I had been a part when I had started dancing, has moved away from me and I am standing alone in the dead centre of what is now my 'dance floor'. My host, the guy who had dragged me here in the first place, is standing in the corner and laughing his arse off, as are most other people actually. I look neither here nor there and immediately proceed to recharge my glass.

A little later, after getting a little more high on 'fun', I find that I am again part of a group of people like me who are standing with glasses in their hands and are moving their heads to the music while looking longingly at the action unfolding on the dance floor. The ladies are in full flow now, dancing with gusto, shaking their hips, moving their hands, swinging their hair, and occasionally glancing around to check whether the boys are noticing them or not. I see that the 'cooler' boys are putting up a good show as well. Good for them. People are hugging each other, holding hands, occasionally tapping someone on the back, pinching each other's cheeks. I love this openness, and like my friends standing with me, I have only a singular question in my mind: How do *I* become a part of *them* and get away from *here*?

To the first part of the question, I have simply no answer, but the second part, that can be taken care of. I simply move away and go sit with my glass on a bench in the arena after removing the empty bottles and the Uncle Chipps' packets that are littering it.

For some time, I sit alone. The music and my surroundings have pushed me into a trance-like state and I close my eyes. Then, I hear a lovely voice right next to me.

"Are you sleeping, seriously?"

I open my eyes and turn my head to see a girl looking down at me, smiling.

"No, no. Was just thinking of something random."

"Ohh!" She takes a sip of whatever it is that she is drinking from the glass in her hand.

Silence follows.

I have a strong urge to say something, anything, and I force myself to think hard.

"Nice party," I say slowly.

"Ohh yeah . . . It's an awesome party," she says and runs her hands through her hair. She has gorgeous hair, by the way. Long, thick, unruly tresses. "I had been waiting for it for so long!" she continues. Her 'so' is so heavy.

"Oh really?" I look at her questioningly.

"Yeah. The last two weeks have been super hectic. We had these club activities and classes and I had to submit five assignments!" she reports her work schedule like a newsreader and ends it with, "And on top of everything, I broke up with my boyfriend."

Aha. "Ohh. That's sad. I am sorry to hear that." I have heard this line so many times in so many of the movies that I have watched that it has lost all meaning. But maybe, just maybe, I actually feel a little bad for her as she looks down at her hands, looking a little saddened for the briefest of seconds.

"Nah!" She says then, shaking her head. And then, getting up, she almost shouts, "Good riddance!" Then she turns towards me and asks, "Would you like to go outside? The music is so loud here!"

I am taken aback at the request. "Yes, why not!" I say and rise up from the bench to walk with her.

Outside the dorm, there is a lonely dog waiting for the party to end so that someone will feed it the leftovers. We walk past it and go sit on a small lawn near the dorm. Before long, she starts talking about how her relationship had turned boring, how the difficulties of sustaining a long-distance relationship had started to weigh them down, and how her expectations from her boyfriend were not being met. In between the monologue, she is considerate enough to pause and ask, "I hope I am not boring you?"

"No, no. Not at all," I hasten to reassure her. "So you were saying . . ."

"Yes, and so he . . ." and she begins talking again.

This girl is not in my section, but I know about her. She is easily among the best looking girls on the campus. She had interned with a very good company and had later gotten herself a PPO from one of the most coveted companies. She plays volleyball and is also a wonderful actress. Basically, she is just perfect. And she is humble, this I know from what others talk of her. I had never talked to her before this. She is the kind of girl people generally admire and whose being successful in life is taken as a given fact. But, I am having some difficulty in mapping that image of her to the one I am witnessing now. She seems vulnerable and her voice wavers now and then. And even when she uses abusive language to curse her ex-boyfriend, her soft voice makes all the words sound sweet and melodious.

Eventually, I see people begin to leave the party. When they catch sight of us sitting on the lawn and talking, they throw speculative glances at us. She doesn't seem to care, but I begin to feel a little uneasy.

"Can we take a stroll around the campus? I feel like walking!" I suggest, stopping her in the middle of a sentence.

"Ahh! Finally you said something on your own! Without it being an answer to a question! I was beginning to wonder if you would ever do that. You don't seem to speak much, do you?" She smiles at me.

Well, she hadn't given me too many chances to speak! But I can't say that out aloud, can I? So I just laugh back. Both of us get up and start walking. After a brief silence, a comfortable silence, I would say, the focus of the largely one-sided conversation shifts to her dorm mates. For the next half an hour, as we walk through the tunnel which joins the new campus to the old one, cross CT, and sit down at the LKP, she gives me a pretty detailed psychoanalysis of all her dorm mates. By the end of that half hour, I can confidently claim to know a fair bit about their good and bad qualities.

Throughout, the strangeness of the whole situation has been knocking inside my head. And now, as it gets over me, I find myself asking her, "Tell me, do you actually know me?"

She looks stunned, as if I had proposed marriage. Then she shakes her head and says, "What a crappy question! You are from Section G, the silent boy." She stresses on the last two words. And for some reason, I am relieved and a bit happy as well.

She goes silent after this. We share a smoke and both of us keep staring at the giant trees bordering the lawn on the opposite side. The silence is not uncomfortable and I am at ease. Correction, she has put me at ease.

"You have a girlfriend?" she asks a little while later.

"Nope. Never had one."

She looks at me, surprised.

"Don't lie."

"I am not lying. Why would I?"

"That's strange."

"Well, today seems to be the day for strange things!" I quip and both of us burst into laughter.

For a long time, I think about what to say next. But relishing the invisible spark in our silence, I keep mum. Then I remember the movies. I have to get her hand, and then, ever so slowly, I have to keep mine on her, otherwise, it's all but lost! But before I can do anything, she scoots closer to me and lays her head on my shoulders. This is even better!

"I always thought you were very selfish."

"What? Why is that?" I ask, surprised.

"Because you are so inactive in class and during T-Nite and during club activities. You hardly talk to anyone."

"I do my work."

She raises her head and looks at me. Then she laughs out loud, pointing at me as if I had just cracked the joke of the century. I want to kiss her so badly. But I just smile.

"What?!"

"N-n-nothing," she says, gasping as she tries to control her laughter. "That was probably the best reply you could have given!"

I shrug my shoulders. She is looking at me with gleaming eyes and a smile on her face. There could have been an invitation in that look. I raise my hands and reach towards her hair so that I can pull her closer to me, but her phone rings right at that instant. Cinematic, much? She darts a quick look at me. She knows that I was about to kiss her. Maybe she is taken aback by how far things have reached, but she drops her phone while taking it out of her bag.

It is one of her friends. They are chilling at CT. She decides to go there and join them. I hated to leave, to end the night so abruptly, but she says, "I umm... have to go now. My friends are a bit worried . . . I walked out of the party without telling them . . ." she trails off. I nod my head in response. I mean, what could I have possibly said anyway?

"Would you like to join us?" she asks after an endlessly long minute. The invitation sounds a bit cold, I feel. Maybe things have dawned upon her and she wants to get away. Maybe she regrets the whole night. But I say yes and we head together to CT.

The moment we join them, she becomes a part of them. Her vulnerabilities vanishes into thin air. Her sensibilities change, and she becomes the girl I have heard of, the confident, friendly, and sure-of-herself woman. The girl I had spent the last few hours with, she all but disappears.

Even her friends are not of my 'frequency' as they say. They laughed at jokes which she and I had made fun of and dissed completely only an hour back. They are good people, but the loss I have suffered by agreeing to come to CT and end my evening with her, it is too big for me to continue sitting there and pretend that I am enjoying their company. When I am sure that it is over for me, I get up from my chair.

"I am leaving. See you guys."

They all look up at me and nod their heads. "Bye. Take care!" one by one they call out.

But she does not say anything. She just gives me a weak smile. I notice a hint of gloom on her face. Or maybe it is simply wishful thinking on my part.

Walking back towards my dorm, I tell myself that I should go back to the room and sit and think about what the hell happened to me. And maybe, I can imagine how it could have ended differently if that damn phone hadn't rung.

Just then, I hear somebody shouting my name. I turn back to see her running towards me, her hand held out in front of her. She has something in her hand and she is waving it wildly. I did not want to show it, but I am elated to see her again, that too, alone.

She is huffing and puffing by the time she reaches me.

"You, you forgot your wallet," she says in between laboured breaths. "You had kept it on the table."

I take my wallet from her, secretly thanking my forgetfulness this one time.

"Thanks," I say, trying to appear as nonchalant about things as I can manage.

There is silence between us again, and this time it's an uncomfortable one. She has her hands on her waist and is leaning forward a little, still trying to catch her breath. Slowly, a minute or two later, she straightens and raises her eyes up to my face. I stare directly into her eyes, as if pouring out all my emotions into that one look. She would surely have realised by now that I was beginning to like her.

And then, in an even stranger chain of events, she looks around the empty path, comes closer to me, takes one deep breath, plants a kiss on my lips, whispers goodbye, and turns around and walks back briskly in the direction she had come from.

All of this happens in a flash and I have no time to react. I stand there for some time and watch her disappear into the darkness.

Eventually, I manage to walk back slowly to my room, unlock the door, and quietly crawl into bed, still dressed in my clothes and with my shoes on. It was my first kiss. I had seen so many of them in the movies. I had heard about it from my friends. I had read about it in the books. But nothing, nothing at all, had prepared me for the full impact of the moment when it actually happened to me. If I could, I would have probably gone back to the moment and changed the way I had stood staring after her like a mute baboon in the aftermath of the kiss. I would have grasped her hand, swept her off her feet, and drawn out that kiss until the end of eternity. But I can't, can I? She gave me this gift, wrapped in a feeling of sweetness and joy, and I know all I can do is savour and save the feelings I experienced in that moment for the rest of my life.

Bite Me

SIDDHARTHA BHASKER

The dogs of the IIMA campus were deep in contemplation. Rumours had been confirmed. The institute was taking serious action to get rid of each and every one of them, once and for all. Yes, the rumours had been going around since the time of their forefathers, but apart from a few roadblocks here and there, life on campus had been peaceful. Maybe not anymore!

"How are you so sure that we will be evacuated?" asked an elder dog, the leader of the pack, in a concerned tone.

"Furry overheard it," one of the younger dogs replied. "Two professors were discussing this during their morning walk."

"Is he sure?"

"Yes, yes. He followed them throughout, keeping as close to them as possible without raising any doubts."

Furry was the only dog on campus with fur. With the temperatures of Ahmedabad being close to moderate, the reasons and utility of having fur were always a topic of debate. But genes play their own little games. Like they did with Pinku. Pinku was sickly thin, and one always got the impression that he would fall down any moment, not that he did . . .

"Call the others as well," the old dog said after a minute of silence. "Let's have a meeting near the Harvard Steps."

"Yes, Leader," the two younger dogs replied in unison and went running to inform the others.

Meanwhile, a hot debate was raging within the IIMA community, with mails over mails being written on what measures should be taken to tackle the 'dog menace', as they called it. The instances of dogs biting people on the campus had increased considerably. So much so that Apollos[8] was doing brisk business from selling anti-rabies' injections.

The community, however, was divided. While the majority seemed to be in favour of removing

---

8   Apollos is the name of the pharmacy inside the IIMA campus.

the dogs from the campus entirely, there were a few animal lovers who opposed this. Both sides had their arguments ready, but no consensus had been reached yet. And the dogs knew this, they had their sources.

***

All the dogs of the campus were in attendance in the meeting in the small lawn touching the Harvard Steps. Concern was written large and clear on their faces. The leader among them was sitting right in the centre of the pack. He took a look around and then started speaking.

"Does anybody have any ideas about how we should act?"

"We need a strategy," somebody said from the back of the pack.

"A marketing strategy to be precise. We need to brand ourselves as being useful to society. We have gathered too many negative reviews. A control and revival of our brand is the need of the hour." The dog who said this was Thor, generally found roaming around the new CR buildings where the classes of the first-year students were held.

"Control is important, I agree," said one of the elder dogs, nodding her head. "Our youth is going astray. Why have so many people been bitten recently?" she asked, looking pointedly at the younger members of the pack.

"And who the hell bit the professor's son, huh?" demanded another elder dog in anger. "We have followed a clear-cut policy of staying away from the administrative staff, the professors, and their children. Target the students. Period."

"Seriously, guys. Our positioning is not correct, not correct at all!" a third elderly dog dispersed his wisdom.

"Ah policies, positioning, strategies! All these globe words that you elderlies have learnt and are trying to impose upon us!" shouted Aston, one of the most hot-headed dogs amongst the younger ones. "Why should we restrict our market to only students? In fact, penetration is easier towards the professors' quarters. Plus, they are easier targets too! The students, on the other hand, have now become aware and reactionary. They hit us."

The debate between the elderly dogs and the youth raged on with no clear resolution being visible. On the other side of the fence, the human community was also struggling to reach a conclusive decision. A rather peculiar suggestion had appeared in the discussion that had unfolded over the long mail thread—someone had suggested that the institute buy dog repellents, a new technology which worked much like how mosquito repellents worked. The contraption, in this case, consisted of a chain of rectangular slabs with some weird signal-producing capabilities that would drive dogs away. These slabs needed to be installed at strategic places all around the campus. The placement of the slabs was to be decided using a shortest-path low-cost algorithm which would ensure that the dogs wouldn't have a place to hide in. They would be bombarded with signals wherever they went. The technology, however, was Chinese, and because a handful of people of the community had not had a good experience while using Chinese products, there was a modicum of resistance to the proposal. Someone pointed to her experience with Chinese watches. She said that if a new Chinese watch remained operational for three days, it would live long, otherwise it would stop working in a day or two. The same, she said, could be true for these dog-repelling devices as well. And so the discussion continued for a while longer.

The dogs, meanwhile, had already gathered information about the technology.

"Who is writing the algorithm?"

"Professor X of the Production and Quantitative Management Department."

"Then he will definitely make it tough for us. I have heard him teach. He's a tough cookie . . ."

"Let's bite him. That will send a strong signal. Or

maybe we should just scare him by stalking his family. I know where he lives."

"That could be counterproductive. He might just end up writing the best algorithm of his life. You know how humans work best under pressure."

"It's a shame that these humans have evolved into such intelligent beings. Earlier, their ideas about how to get rid of us were so simple. Once, I remember, a big shot political dignitary was supposed to visit the campus and all of us were packed off to some strange place a little distance away from the campus. Nothing permanent came of it. We just walked back into the campus the next day!"

Even as the dogs nodded their heads and talked amongst themselves, they all looked really scared. Uncertainty was never good, be it in investments or in existence. And unfortunately, given the situation, they couldn't avoid either. Something had to be done to reduce the risk.

"The municipal corporation has given us some rights, hasn't it?" one of the younger dogs asked. "Does anybody remember any of them?"

Stan came forward and explained the laws under which an institution could treat stray animals found within its campus. The laws defined the boundaries of the actions that individuals and institutions could take against animals. Can't do this, can't do that, etc., etc.

"It says nothing about these kinds of technologies though . . . does it?"

"Nope," Stan replied.

"Well," the leader of the pack finally intervened now. Having heard what each member of the pack had to say, it was time for him to set down the action plan. "Let's do a few things. First, let's lie low. Stop biting people, stop chasing people, all of you. If the security guards give us any signal, if they tell us to go away or sit or leave them alone, let's follow it meekly and without any aggressive reactions. Got it?"

Most of the dogs nodded in agreement, although there were murmurs of dissatisfaction that could be heard from the younger ones. "I hate security guards," one whispered to his neighbour. "Will bite a few of them someday for sure."

"And one more thing," the leader continued, glaring at the younger lot. "Some of the humans love us and want us to be here. They are the good ones, our friends. Let's make sure we have their sympathy with us at all times. I am sure all of us know of a few good ones like that . . . Let's memorise their names and remember their faces so that all of us know them. Go to them whenever they are in sight, wag your tail, look at them with your cute little eyes, lick them, roll around in front of them. Do whatever it takes to make them go 'awwwww' and 'oooooh'. But, don't you dare open your mouth in front of them and bare your teeth until you are very very sure they want you to. Some of them like to put their hands inside our mouths and take pictures. Weird as this may seem to us, let them do it. Be sensitive to them. Do everything you can to make sure they stand on our side."

Meanwhile, although a consensus had seemed well within sight when the discussion among the humans of IIMA had first started, now the thread was growing like a distorted bubble with more and more people joining in. A lot of arguments and counterarguments had already been presented. Somebody had floated a form where the residents were asked to vote either in favour of or against the presence of dogs on campus. As expected, more than 90 per cent wanted them out. A group of volunteers was pressurising the authorities to install the dog repellent technology. On mail, people had provided the phone numbers of the important officers of the municipal corporation. Someone had requested the General Secretary of IIMA to talk to them, which he had promised to do. And so it was that the matter was becoming more and more convoluted with every passing day.

The dogs had stayed true to the modus operandi their leader had devised. They stayed as inconspicuous as possible. Nobody bit anybody. And whenever they saw a 'friendly', they made sure they were nothing but adorable little balls of fur and pure love. As a last word of warning, their leader had said that in case anybody got any further updates about the technology the humans were thinking of using or if anyone saw any signs of its implementation on the campus, they were to inform him immediately. Some emergency measures would need to be initiated in such a scenario, although, truth be told, nobody was sure what these 'emergency measures' would be.

But as the days passed and nothing happened, the dogs sensed their enemy retreating. They still carried on with their battle plan, but it was with a heart that was beginning to breathe just a little bit easy. A few days later, two elderly dogs were casually having a chat in the morning on the cricket field.

"So much for the drama that day," one of them commented with a smirk. "We couldn't even take a peaceful stroll anywhere, lest a dog hater saw us and complained to the authorities. What a mess!"

"True, true . . ." the other one commiserated. "What happened to the technology thing?"

"Guess it was not meant to happen. Hey, look!" He pointed towards the running track where they saw their leader sitting upright, his brows furrowed in intense attention as he stared at a guy running on the track, dressed in an eye-catching yellow tee-shirt and a pair of black shorts. Even from the distance, the two dogs could sense that something was going to happen from the menace in the eyes of their leader. The runner, after a slow start, increased his speed in the second lap. As the dogs watched with bated breath, he came closer and closer to where their leader was sitting right on the track, clearly biding his time. Would this moment be an announcement of their resurrection as a tribe?

The runner was oblivious to the impending danger. He was closing in on the leader and just when he was one leap away, the unfortunate boy exchanged a brief glance with the leader. It worked as a signal, that one glance, and the predator pounded upon the boy's thighs as if they were raw meat and pierced them with his powerful teeth. The runner cried out, a deathly scream that was loud enough to reach the farthest of dorms and make many stop right in their tracks and shudder. He fell down on the track the next second, clutching his leg, blood oozing out from the wound. The leader gave him one long look, enough to put the fear of God in him forever, and walked away like a triumphant king. After a few minutes, the boy rose up and hobbled his way to the nearest KLMDC building to wash the wounds, leaving a trail of blood on the tracks as he went.

"And that's why he is our leader . . ." one of the elder dogs commented in a whisper as they watched the boy disappear into the building.

"Yeah . . . Poor boy though . . ."

"Don't worry, he'll get the injections and be just fine. But thankfully, things will come back to normal again now. So much for the discussion!"

Chakru Clears His Debts

CHAKRU

◦∞◦

Chakru came from a family in debt. Ever since he was a child, debtors would often turn up at his house and demand that their loans be repaid. Some of them would even abuse his father. On most days, Chakru saw his father depressed and his mother anxious. They were constantly worried about making ends meet because try as he might, Chakru's father was never able to make things work. All his business ventures failed one after the other, and on those rare occasions when he found a job, he was never able to retain it for more than a month or two. And so Chakru grew up with parents who loved him but who were unable to resolve the tension and the sense of instability that was palpable in their house.

But penury doesn't affect parental aspirations. Chakru's parents wanted him to get into an IIT and find himself a high-paying job. 'Engineering' was the magic word for them; it would solve all their troubles once and for all. Chakru found himself cycling 25 kms to Patna every day to get to a good tuition that would prepare him for the entrance exams. He put all his energy into the preparations. The wish to make his parents happy had taken deep roots in his heart and would just not leave him. But God had other plans. Chakru did not clear the entrance exam for IIT and ended up going to an engineering college in the southern parts of the country where it was difficult for him to understand the English the professors spoke. Truth be told, they couldn't understand his English either.

Even as despair set in, the burning desire to get his parents out of debt never died. One day, while Chakru was reading the newspaper in his hostel common room, he read about students of IIMA securing high packages, sometimes as high as a crore, in their campus placements. The flame was rekindled. He started preparing hard for the CAT exam. Day and night, he would read books about quantitative aptitude and logical reasoning. He would solve problems, work his way through test series, and pray fervently to the gods above to get him into IIMA. This time, the gods were listening.

He got in!

The initial days were a shock to his system, no doubt. The sheer burden of the things he was expected to already know would have sent him crumbling to his knees, if not the weight of the course itself. But Chakru persisted. And as the days passed, he settled in. Eventually, in spite of the hectic schedule of the place and the insane levels of competition among his peers, he took out the time to play cricket, dance during T-Nite, take part in a lemon race, act in a street play, and fall in love (although that didn't really lead anywhere). He used to play poker in undergraduate college and the itch to get back into the game got the better of him when he heard about the poker games being held in some dorms on campus. He became a regular at these poker games and eventually came to be touted as a sort of poker champion. He made lots of friends during these games, many of whom overwhelmed him with their achievements. But through it all, he kept an eye on that astronomical salary he wanted.

When the time came for his batch to actually go after their dream jobs and salaries, the preparations started with innumerable rounds of meetings with the CV mentors and company visits in addition to truckloads of assignments and surprise quizzes. Everyone was asked to prepare a master CV, which was to showcase everything they had done in their lives so far, ranging from a fancy dress competition they might have taken part in in Class 2 to being a Chartered Financial Analyst Level-3 scholar. The bigger and fatter your CV, the better chances you had to score the package you had lusted after. A mad race ensued as Chakru's peers scrambled to get approvals from their professors and from the managers of companies they had worked for during their summer internships. People were having a hard time convincing their managers about how they had saved more than five crores during their short stint of 2.37 months in the company and how they were part of the core organising team of the international fest in their college even though all they had actually done was move three chairs from one of the classrooms to the auditorium.

When Chakru's CV mentor asked him to meet up, Chakru went with a half-page CV which had some sparse details, that too all disarranged, and some vague unverified points. The fuming mentor threatened Chakru: "I am going to complain to the PlaceComm coordinator unless you whip this piece of shit into shape!" That literally made Chakru shit in his pants as PlaceComm deadlines were considered sacrosanct and tampering with them meant literal death. The dreams that Chakru had of pocketing fat pay cheques all came crashing down. Reality hit him like a speeding truck. Chakru knew he had to get his act together. The next few weeks, therefore, were spent talking to his school teachers to get some recommendation, some words of value out of them (no proof of any merit was coming from his college; he had tried and failed) and sorting out his emails to find something worth it in them. The past sin of not participating in events which provided certificates now kept haunting him. Somehow, however, he reconfigured his CV into something which, according to him, could be easily deemed as one of the most undeserving CVs ever, yet something which somehow managed to barely pass muster.

The shortlists started pouring in very soon, and the corridors of their dorms rang with applause for people who had made it into the high-paying consultancy firms and the investment banks. After a while, Chakru stopped checking the shortlists because his name had not even appeared at the bottom of a single list even after more than fifteen shortlists had come and gone. At one point in time, Chakru began contemplating the idea of not falling for this mad race after money and simply quitting the placement process by taking up an internship in an NGO. He discussed this with his friend Bobby (who had made it to almost every shortlist there was, obviously) and he said, very passionately so, that putting up a fight against the oddest of odds was the norm in corporate culture. Chakru had to fight. There was no other way out of this. Bobby's fiery speech instilled a new sense of self-belief in Chakru. Further affirmation came when he found his name on the shortlist for an investment bank the next day. His happiness knew no bounds and though the chances of conversion were very less, it gave him a reason to celebrate after a long time. Poor grades, a harrowing meeting with his CV mentor, and the zero-shortlist count had all but drained him out entirely. Time whizzed right past him as he spent night after night preparing for the interview, and then came D-day. Chakru found himself sitting right next to his love in the last row, with both of them having only a single shortlist to boast of. Could this be an omen of good things to come, the boy wondered, sneaking a glance at her tightly clenched fists. But watching the shops of the companies closing very fast after they found suitable candidates, that tiny flicker of hope sort of, well, it died. Eventually, after missing lunch and sitting through five hours of continuous expectations, they were told that the selection process for that day was over and they were required to head back to their dorms and prepare for the gruelling schedule of the upcoming days when more rounds of placements would take place. Chakru, quite clearly, didn't get through the bank.

Group Discussion (GD) was on the agenda for

the next day and Chakru really really sucked in them. GD rooms were like live battlefields. Friendships were forgotten in GD rooms, as were loyalties and loves, and all that remained was cut-throat competition for the fancy job at stake. Chakru had about seven or eight shortlists for GD, but owing to his lack of accented English and his inability to stand out in the room, he was rejected in all, one by one. By late night, more than fifty companies had come out with their interview schedules for the next day and Chakru, needless to say, featured in none of them. It was one of the most difficult nights for Chakru. He silently cursed everybody around him and as negative thoughts slowly engulfed him, he even considered the option of doing something really undesirable.

All of a sudden, the phone rang, forcing him to snap out of his misery. 'Mummy calling', it said on the screen. He didn't want to talk to anyone, but this was a call he couldn't ignore. So he picked up the call and cried his heart out. His mother, the sensible woman that she was, consoled him quietly and literally brought him back from the edge of the precipice he had pushed himself into. The negative thoughts dispersed one after the other and Chakru found himself in a slightly better place.

The next day, he was sitting in the last row again, hiding his face, when someone from the front of the classroom took his name and instructed him to go for the interview round with Moon Radio. Chakru got up slowly, disbelief writ large and clear on his face. But he knew that this was the moment to seize. He went into the interview room all smiling despite a sunken heart beating dully within his ribcage, and maintained a jolly composure throughout. The interview was, much to his surprise, pretty eventful and strange. The man from Moon Radio didn't ask him anything about Maslow hierarchy or Internal Rate of Returns. Instead, the questions ranged from trivia about *Kaun Banega Crorepati* to the analysis of a Bollywood movie. It was right up Chakru's alley, and he knew he had done well in the interview. When the job was offered to him, he was, simply put, ecstatic.

He called his parents in the evening. His father was overwhelmed with joy, stammering and fumbling over his words, while his mother just started crying. Chakru told them that with the package he had bagged, he could clear their debts in one year straight. After that, he would buy a house for them in Patna. He specifically asked his father to give him the phone numbers of their debtors. He said he would call them one by one and assure them that their money would be returned, with interest, over the next one year. The conversation with his parents was a long, emotional one. And though he was himself in tears by the time he kept the phone, he made one last phone call before calling it a night.

He called his love. It seems that five hours of sitting together, each caught in a web of deep despair, had caused certain shifts. The winds of love, if one can call them that, appeared to have started blowing ever so gently.

After that, Chakru went to sleep. It was something he had been looking forward to all his life: a sleep devoid of anxiety, a sleep that is sweet, peaceful, and filled with youthful hope.

DiscF

PHD WALLAH

∽∞∽

"Everything in this place is for the MBAs. It's as if we, the FPMs[9] do not have an existence. As if we are ghosts!" said Parkhi, running her hands through her black curly hair, something she was in the habit of doing when she was even a tad agitated.

"Why don't you join us in forming the Discussion Forum (DiscF)?" I asked her. "It's a discussion forum that we are creating for the FPMs. A club of sorts, if you will . . ."

"What will this club do?"

---

9   Fellow Program in Management students or the PhD students on the campus.

"Well . . . let's see . . . the club would hold weekly discussions on a pre-decided topic, and the members can see if they can come up with some new, exciting topics for research and collaboration . . ."

"Too fancy for me," Parkhi said, shaking her head. "You guys go ahead. I am happy with my fiction. In any case, one single club cannot change what this place smells like—a heaven for the MBAs and a dungeon for the FPMs."

"Hope you change your mind though!" I called out as I waved her goodbye and crossed the underground passage that led towards the new campus. Parkhi lived in the old campus dorms. She was a thin, short woman with a great love for salwar kameez. She had innumerable sets of them in all possible colours, and in all the time that I had known her, I had never seen her dressed in anything else but a salwar kameez. Another thing she had an undying love for was earrings. In fact, her room was full of earrings of all shapes and sizes—one could find earrings lying on her study table, her bed, in between her books, inside her bag, amidst a pile of laundry waiting to be folded and kept inside her cupboard, inside a spare coffee mug, and just about everywhere else. And she loved fiction. Vehemently so. Sylvia Plath, Hillary Mantel, and Alice Munro were her favourites. Parkhi was, to put it simply, quite the character.

Once back in my own dorm, I took a shower. The sun had been shining hard outside and my clothes were drenched in sweat. After that, I called Ruby on the intercom. A fellow FPM scholar, she was helping me create DiscF.

"Hi, hope I am not disturbing you?"

"No, no. Not at all. I was just cleaning my room."

"Should we meet today then? We have to chalk out a plan for the first session na . . ."

"Sure thing. Let's meet in the library?"

"Yes, works. At 7:00 pm then."

"Done. Bye!"

The library reading room was quiet when we got there. The chairs were mostly empty and the big wooden tables stood in peace, with no towering piles of books cluttering them. Ruby and I were soon immersed in making a rough draft of sorts on my laptop. As usual, she was the one giving ideas about how we should structure the first session of our club. Ruby was around my age. With a Greek nose that dominated her face and long hair that always looked unruly no matter how much she combed it, she had a slow and deliberate way of speaking that instantly put people at ease and made everyone want to listen to what she was saying. She had become my partner in a short time in the creation of the club. We were working on the presentation we were going to make in the first session of DiscF. We had no idea really, about how many FPM scholars would turn up for the session. Some of them had shown interest, while most others had simply walked away when we had pitched the idea to them. The session was scheduled for the next day and we had already booked a classroom for it.

After our presentation was ready, we went to CT to have tea. Parkhi was sitting there with some of her friends. Spotting me, she came over to sit with us.

"So, what bomb are you guys going to detonate tomorrow?" she asked, grinning.

"You'll see it tomorrow. We've got a pretty lethal arsenal!" Ruby shot back.

"I am not really interested," Parkhi said, shaking her head. "Nothing will come out of it."

"Why are you so negative, Parkhi? You can at least cheer us up even if you don't wish to attend the first session, no?"

"Haha! Cheer you up? For what? Forget these things man, and just listen to the songs of *Fitoor*! God, they are bliss."

We talked for a while after that about the new movie *Fitoor*, which was about to be released. After a while, I parted company, had my dinner in the mess, went back to my room, read a little, and then went to sleep.

The next evening, after our classes got over, we

met for our first session of DiscF. Around ten people had turned up, which wasn't all that bad, all things considering. We presented our inaugural statement and then laid out our plan for the structure of the club. There was active participation from everybody and we finally ended up reaching a consensus about the structure of the club and decided that we would meet biweekly. The topic of discussion for the next session was to be circulated over email by Ruby and me. It was, all in all, an auspicious start.

Over the next few weeks, DiscF sessions took off with a bang. More and more people joined in. FPM students would randomly stop me on the campus and give me suggestions about how to steer the sessions, what to add, and what to remove. Some of them said the faculty should be invited. Some suggested that research papers should be the focus of the discussions. There was such a great variety of ideas being thrown at Ruby and me that I started getting irritated whenever anyone stopped me and offered unsolicited advice. I started telling them to attend the sessions and present their ideas there in front of everyone instead of pitching them to me or Ruby individually.

In all of this, Parkhi, however, did not budge. I never saw her in any of the sessions even though word about DiscF had spread across the campus literally like wildfire. I met her after a few weeks. She was sitting at the edge of the football field and watching the first-year MBAs play the second-year MBAs.

"The first-year team is good this time," she said as I sat down beside her. "We will have a fighting team for Sangharsh.[10]"

"Is that so? A gold perhaps?"

"It depends on how the other teams are."

There was a brief silence as we looked at the forward of the second-year team come close to scoring a goal. He gave it a good kick, but the ball hit the goal post and bounced back.

"Damn!" Parkhi muttered under her breath. "I hear DiscF is going well," she said, turning towards me. "Congratulations. You seem to have lit a glimmer of light in this godforsaken program."

"Wow. That's quite a change in opinion!" I exclaimed. Curious, I peered at her and asked, "So . . . you think there is hope?"

"No, I didn't say that," Parkhi laughed, promptly bursting my bubble. "I said you have lit a flame. Am pretty sure though that it's going to fizzle out in some time. Until you have the MBA tag, you won't find anyone being enthusiastic about anything in this place."

"One can always try!"

---

10 The name of the inter-IIM sports festival.

"Oh, there is nothing wrong in trying. But people should care as well, don't you think?"

"People do care, Parkhi," I protested. "Our attendance is increasing with every session. Our debates are becoming livelier!"

"Well, good luck to you then!"

And that was the end of our conversation that day.

Meanwhile, the club had gathered speed. Before every session, we picked up a book or a topic of discussion and people would nominate someone from amongst the members to lead the sessions. In the first session that week, we had picked up the book *Small is Beautiful* by EF Schumacher for discussion. The members had split up into two groups, one in support of the ideas in the book, the other against it. The former group read passages from the book and emphasised how the current thinking in economics was not suitable for the world, especially for a country like India. The other group, standing in opposition, highlighted the achievements of neoliberal economics by talking about several macroeconomics initiatives which had pulled countries out of poverty. The moderator for the session, a girl named Apoorva, was having difficulty controlling the debate as passions began to fly high. Many of the FPM scholars wanted to speak but people were hardly in the mood to listen. Everyone just wanted to drive their own point home. Two scholars, in particular, were especially at each other's throats and it looked like they would pounce on each other in no time!

While the session ended without there being a bloodbath, the MBAs came to know of our club sessions as well. Some of them came up to us and said they wanted to attend the club meetings. Needless to say, we had no problems. The more the better. In fact, things got to such a point that the institute itself arranged for tea and snacks for us! DiscF had now truly arrived on campus! Even as the club became a central meeting point for all the FPMs on campus, most importantly, it was something that kept me engaged. The only thing which worried me was Parkhi's nonchalant attitude towards these sessions. Her independent views and her presence would have been a good addition to the debates, but I had no idea how to get her interested. I met her often enough in the cafeteria, and we spoke frequently about what was happening with DiscF, but she never budged from her decision to not attend the sessions. One day, I found her reading a book at CT.

"What is this showing off?" I asked, plonking down on the chair next to hers and pointing at the book in her hand.

"This is not showing off. This is pleasure."

"Ah! The pleasure of letting others know that you read, is it?" I retorted.

"The pleasure of reading with a cup of decent coffee beside you and with the wind blowing in your hair!"

"Pffft! Don't give me that. We have coffee in our DiscF sessions. And there's enough wind blowing from the mouths of those passionate zealots, if you know what I mean . . ."

"Don't get me started on your DiscF. It's all glitter and no gold."

"You cannot produce gold without there being some heat! Tell me, what will it take for you to come to at least one of our sessions?"

"Research ideas. Good research ideas. That is what I would love. After all, that's what we have to do, no? Produce good research?"

"You know good ideas arise out of discussions on books and when you engage in debates on different topics, right?"

"Never," Parkhi shook her head. "The way things are here, no good ideas will ever come out of anything. Unless, of course, it is related to something that's trending in the West. We Indians don't have an eye for originality. We love aping the West. This whole institute, in fact, is a copy of institutes in the West. I do not want to partake in anything which is not original. As it is we were inextricably tied to the ghost of the West the day we stepped foot inside this institute."

I felt a slight repugnance towards her attitude. "Science and knowledge are things that exist in the public sphere. There is nothing West or East about them."

"You are wrong there, my dear friend. The 'science' that we have here is Western science. And we are being trained brilliantly to ape the West. That is what will get us high-paying jobs. Tell me of even one original idea that has come out of any of the numerous PhD theses that this institute has published? It has been operative for more than fifty years, right? Shouldn't we have seen at least one groundbreaking study come from this institute by now?"

I had never heard of any idea or paper from any PhD scholar, past or present, which had really changed anything in the field of social science. I kept quiet.

"So, if you want me to come to DiscF, I want to be sure that you guys are not just blind copycats building something that is based entirely on the Western structures of organic academic engagement, which, unfortunately, is mostly what your baby is going to turn out to be . . ."

We parted a little after that, and although I didn't see Parkhi for the next couple of days, her arguments kept running in my mind. Parkhi had never disappointed me when it came to her sharp insight into things. I knew that I had not been inspired by any Western structures or systems of thought while creating DiscF. It was, in my opinion, an organic creation which would take a more concrete shape and form over time as more and more people engaged with it and influenced its course. But from what Parkhi told me, it didn't look like we were actually creating an organic space where an original idea could take birth. Far from it. All we were doing was picking up a topic or a theme and holding discussions and debates around it. We were picking up hypotheses and either proving them right or disapproving them. Nobody took things any further. It was quite apparent that Parkhi's arguments held merit.

I decided to bring about a few changes in the way DiscF operated. Ruby agreed with me, and we announced it in the next session. DiscF would be more about ideas from now on. We would engage with current questions and gaps in research which could be worked into original research papers later if any of the PhD scholars wanted to take them up. Collaboration was encouraged as well. While a few people nodded their heads in agreement, I heard quite a few disgruntled voices as well.

For the next session, I said, I would take the lead and discuss the Gale-Shapley stable marriage algorithm since I wished to work on it further. I urged the others to read up on the subject and come. That whole week, I read paper after paper on the matching algorithm. I was surprised to read that Lloyd Shapley had come up with a solution for stable marriage within one day.

A day before the session, I met Parkhi and during the course of our conversation, I told her about the changes we were bringing about in DiscF. She smiled when she heard me, but she didn't ask any questions about it or discuss it further.

The next day, only a few people attended the session. Clearly, after my announcement about the changes in DiscF's agenda, the attendance had decreased. Some of the regular FPMs had probably decided to give up. Determined to plough on, I didn't let the dwindling numbers affect me, and started the session with an introduction to the Gale-Shapley algorithm. I was explaining the stable marriage problem when I heard someone come running down the corridor just outside the classroom. Then, the door to the classroom opened. And there stood Parkhi in a yellow salwar kameez, huffing and puffing as she tried to catch her breath. She looked at me a little apologetically for being late, and then quietly slipped in and took a seat at the last bench. I gave her the briefest of nods and resumed talking. I was happy. DiscF was clearly on the right track now.

The Taxi Driver

AKSHIT SHARMA

~~~

"What does the crow understand about the pain a buffalo experiences as it slowly devours the flesh off its back?" boomed the *kaali-peeli* (black and yellow) Fiat taxi driver in a crisp American accent as we sped through the narrow lanes of Colaba towards Church Gate.

I had very recently developed a strange love for Mumbai, all thanks to my occasional work trips to the city from Ahmedabad. Mumbai was like a microorganism, always evolving, always taking on strange shapes and contours, and always so dynamic. I looked outside the taxi window as we drove past Marine Drive, my head still in an altered state of consciousness from an evening well spent. There had been a potpourri of people, sounds, lights, smells, and emotions that I had experienced. It had literally felt like I had rushed through a thousand paintings in some art gallery, each one so unique, so immense in itself, but each offering just a glimpse, just a teaser into the lives it depicted.

My train of thought was interrupted by the driver's loud remark. I snapped back to the present and looked ahead through the windshield to see an Audi crisscrossing through the traffic, being a nuisance on the road. It must have overtaken our taxi at about the same time when the driver had yelled. And then it hit me: the driver's English was quite impressive, his enunciation clear, and the thought too profound. I was curious to ask him where he'd learnt English so well, but I did not quite know how to phrase the question. "At least we love life and let it love us back!" the man continued to speak. I looked hard to get a better view of the driver's face, but could not—it was still dark.

I tried to zone out again, looking outside the window once more, but my thoughts got the better of me. There was clearly something unusual about this taxi driver, especially his manner of speech. My thoughts, as expected, then drifted towards the absurd and the fear of the unknown. Why was my taxi driver talking to himself? Or was he imagining someone sitting beside him, listening to him? Perhaps he was in a bad mood. Or maybe he was just a plain old eccentric man? In either case, I should have nothing to fear, I reassured myself. Most people tended to rate my opinions and actions as being on the lower side of the eccentricity spectrum on any given day and I had made my peace with that. Eccentricity was a part of the evolutionary process, I believed. It carried human ideas ahead, for every opinion deemed acceptable now was once dismissed as being eccentric.

We entered the well-lit Marine Drive and went zipping past the streetlights. I saw the shadows inside the taxi grow bigger and bigger, until they faded in a moment, before being reborn again. It was like the rippling of the waves in the sea outside. My mind drifted back to a discussion I had had with a friend earlier, who, in a moment of sudden enlightenment and post-work frustration, spoke about happiness and the human spirit. He had talked about how some people have an infinite human spirit that enables them to not get bogged down by trying circumstances. It's this human spirit that helps them to endure suffering and live a life full of stress while yearning for momentary relief through materialistic pleasures. I had discredited the theory at that time, blaming it on exaggerations conceived in a head filled with smoke and inspired by a bad day at work. But as I looked outside the window, I thought about how right he had been about all of our lives. The strangest of thoughts have a way of coming back at the uncanniest of times. I didn't know at that time what was so peculiar about the situation, but I do know now. Reluctantly, I shook off those thoughts and focused my attention back on my taxi driver.

In the gleaming streetlight, I tried to get a glimpse of the driver again while appearing nonchalant, leaning back into the seat with my head resting against the window frame. He was an old man, probably in his early 70s. His balding head was flanked by patches of white hair on the sides. I looked at the rear-view mirror to catch a better look at his face. The first thing I saw was a pair of John Lennon glasses that went perfectly with the white handlebar moustache dominating his face. That's the second thing I saw, by the way, the moustache, that is. The rest of his face, I couldn't quite catch. He was wearing a white shirt that still looked crisp and freshly starched. Then, as he steered a smooth left, I saw the white gloves on his hands. Who was this man?! My urge for an answer grew stronger. My question, on the other hand, grew hazier.

Suddenly, the quiet that I had been enjoying was broken by a phone's ringtone. It was the driver's phone. He let it ring for what seemed like an eternity. At any other time, I would have asked him to silence that damn thing. But I stayed quiet for some reason that I could not pinpoint and let that annoying ringtone play out.

A few more minutes later, we reached my destination. As he gradually swerved to the side of Marine Drive to let me off, his phone rang again. He let it ring until I got out of the taxi and handed him a fifty rupee note through the window.

Then, our business transaction over and with me turning around to walk away from the road and towards the sea, I heard him pick up the phone and say, "Hello, Mr Patrick! I'm sorry! I was driving earlier . . ."

I was trying to comprehend the whole episode that had seemed so unusual to me. Was it just me who found it a little too perplexing? Or was there really something out of the ordinary about the man? I was still trying to pinpoint the question that I needed the answer to, and the feeling was very unsettling.

Before I realised it, I found myself turning back and walking towards the taxi yet again. The driver had hung up by then, so I put my hands on the front window frame and leaned in.

"I'm quite impressed with your English speaking skills," I said without beating around the bush.

"Well, thank you!" came the prompt reply, almost as if the man had been expecting this.

I was back where I had started. I didn't know how or what to ask next.

"Does that puzzle you?" asked the driver, as if sensing my feelings and rescuing me.

"No, no, not really. It's just not quite every day that one runs into . . ." I found myself at a loss for words. I scrambled to think of all the ways that I could end that sentence without sounding too judgemental.

"An English-speaking taxi driver?" the man finished the sentence for me and laughed. I couldn't help but smile at myself, nodding at his correct assumption.

"Well, you see, this is what I do. Every evening, I like to take out my taxi and drive along this route—from Colaba, all the way along Marine Drive. I sometimes pick up interesting people like you as passengers and have a chat with them as I drive." He did not say it, but I could see he enjoyed this daily drive. "But you were all too quiet and seemed lost in some other world. I didn't want to disturb you."

He raised his white eyebrows above the steel-rimmed glasses as he finished his sentence, and looked at me questioningly. In that brief moment that passed, the question was thrown back at me: why was this man, who clearly seemed to be educated, well-spoken, and so self-confident, driving a taxi on the streets of Mumbai, a *kaali-peeli* Fiat nonetheless? I couldn't quite decide whether he was leading me on for asking him this question or if he wanted me to ask myself why I found everything about him strange. My curiosity, nevertheless, had shot up even more, but I couldn't risk asking that question without sounding dismissive. Courtesy has a way of turning up at places where you least expect it to. I managed a nod and gave him an unconvincing smile.

"I render my services to the US Embassy for a few hours during the day, before the evening traffic starts to clear up a bit. It is what I have been doing for the past eight years . . ."

It had struck me by then that driving a taxi was probably not his primary profession, and my curiosity, which finally got the better of me, was only well received when I blurted out, "How about your family? You have kids?"

"Yes, my kids are back in Goa. That's where I am from actually. Our family owns a resort there, it's right by the sea . . . my sons are running it . . ."

It felt strange. I was exhausted and rattled with all the questions inside my head. A family and a business in a place like Goa. And yet he preferred driving a taxi in the biggest business hub of India? Had his children forsaken him? Or had he forsaken them?

"They're doing quite well, and I go meet them every month," the man said in a reassuring tone, as if sensing my dilemma and wanting to put my mind at ease.

"Ah . . ." I faltered. "Don't you . . . umm . . . get bored here? Don't you feel lonely? This place can make you feel lonely, isn't it?"

"Not at all! For company, I have the beautiful female voice on FM with me!" he chuckled and continued, "A drive along Marine Drive never makes you feel lonely. Sometimes I meet people who are new to Mumbai. A first visit to this megacity can overwhelm you and make you feel lost. I try to make them feel comfortable, try and help them if I can. Other times you have the locals . . . if they wish to talk and share their joys and sorrows with me, I oblige readily. This city gives wings to your dreams, but with it comes the constant fear of falling into an abyss. There are successes, failures, good days, and bad days. I enjoy the stories the people tell. I love this city and I love the work I do here."

He smiled at me and changed the gear of his taxi. It was a signal—the conversation was over and he was ready to get moving. Even I would not have preferred any small talk after that, not that I was bursting with things to say. As I bid the man a farewell with a quick nod and turned once again towards the sea, I thought about how some people can make you challenge the very assumptions on which we base our world, our entire thought system, and make us rethink every single thing.

Yes, some people are like that, and I'm glad I met him.

Acknowledgement

Thanks to Sumit Sonawane, Shuchi Srinivasan, and Nikita Bharadia for their help in encouraging a busy bunch of people to contribute their stories to this collection.

A big thank you to Gayatri Goswami for being a patient editor.

And finally, I would like to thank Shikha Sabharwal of Fingerprint! for her help in bringing the manuscript to light.

ABOUT THE AUTHOR

Siddhartha completed his education from IIT Kharagpur and IIM Ahmedabad. He teaches Economics at the Jindal Global Business School and works in the field of mental health and game theory. He has published a novel, *B Ground West*. He loves reading and cycling. He tweets at @bgroundwest